D0210568

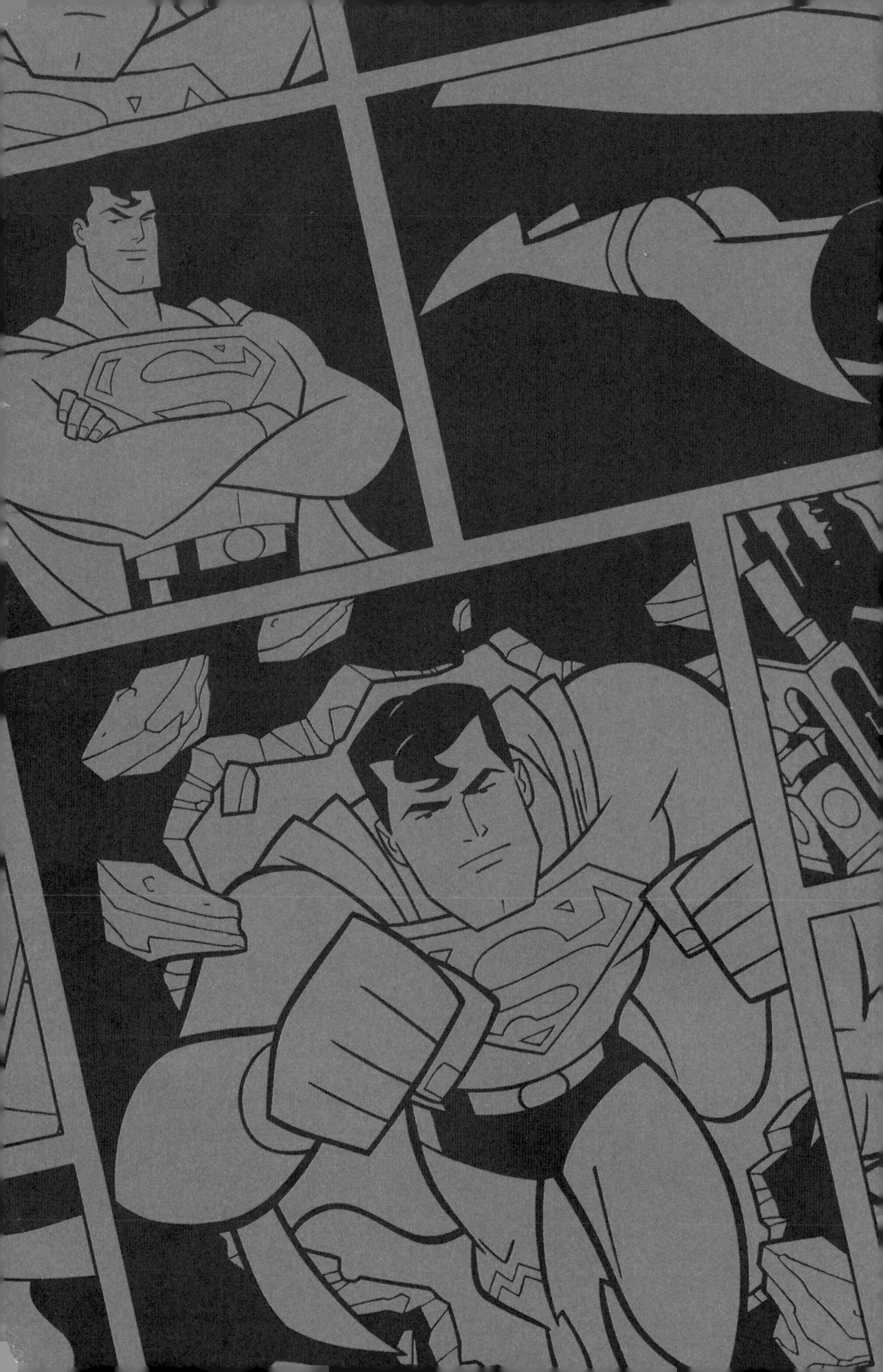

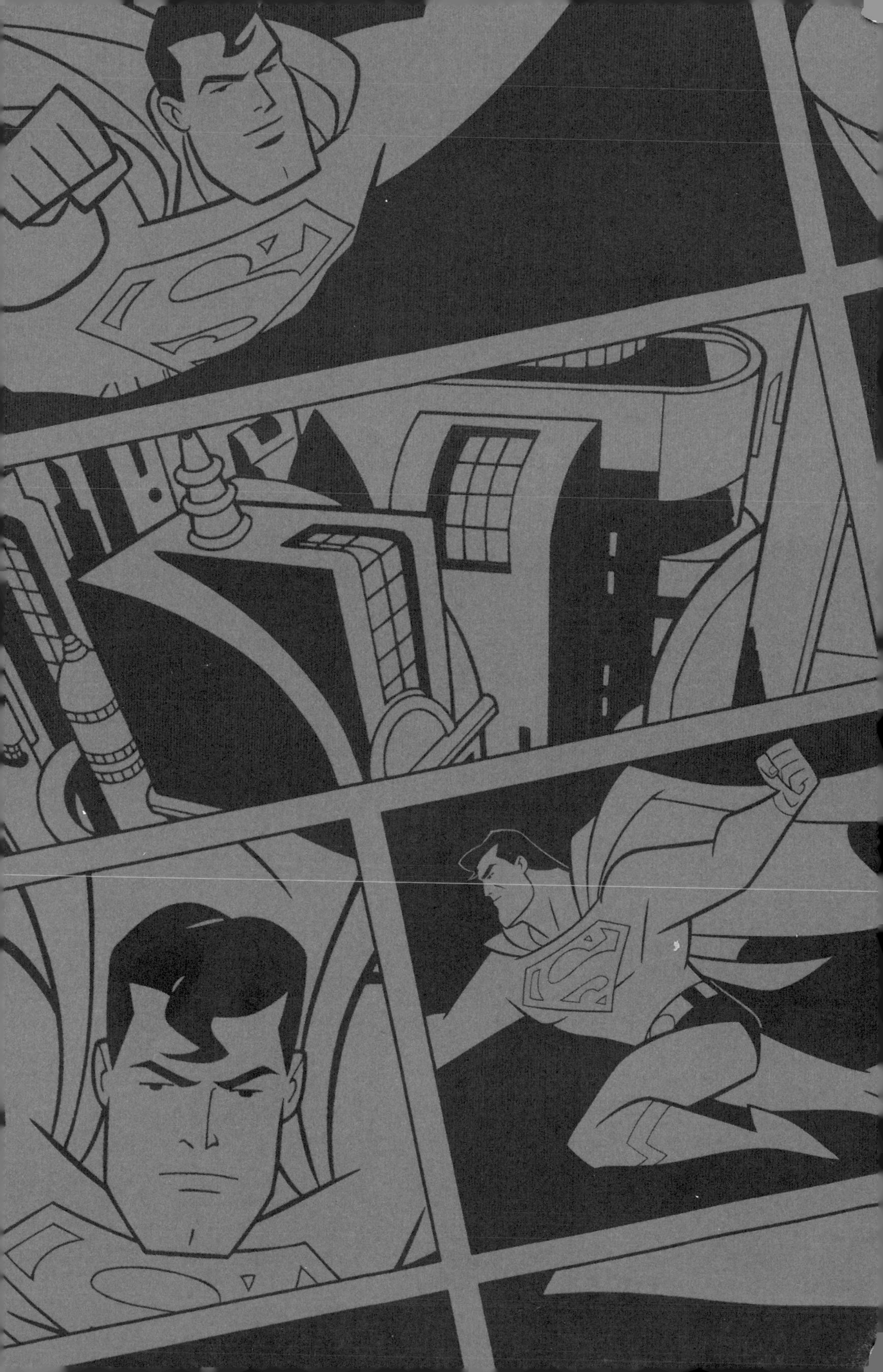

COMIC CHAPTER BOOKS

DC
COMICS™
SUPER
HEROES

SUPERMAN

STONE ARCH BOOKS
a capstone imprint

Superman: Comic Chapter Books are published by
Stone Arch Books,
A Capstone Imprint
1710 Roe Crest Drive
North Mankato, Minnesota 56003
www.capstoneyoungreaders.com

Star33641

Library of Congress Cataloging-in-Publication Data is
available on the Library of Congress website.

ISBN: 978-1-4965-0508-8 (library binding)
ISBN: 978-1-4965-0510-1 (paperback
ISBN: 978-1-4965-2301-3 (eBook)

Summary: Superman has always been a thorn in Lex
Luthor's side, and now Luthor wants the super hero
out of the picture . . . once and for all! The evil super-
genius busts the Parasite out of jail, and the two team
up to make a wicked duo. When Luthor traps the Man
of Steel and the Parasite drains his powers, it looks like
the super-villains may have finally won. Will Superman's
friends Lois Lane and Jimmy Olsen be able to free him,
or is this the last of the world's greatest super hero?

Printed in Canada
052015   008825FRF15

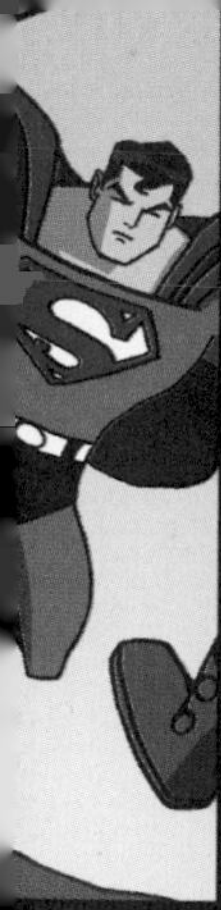
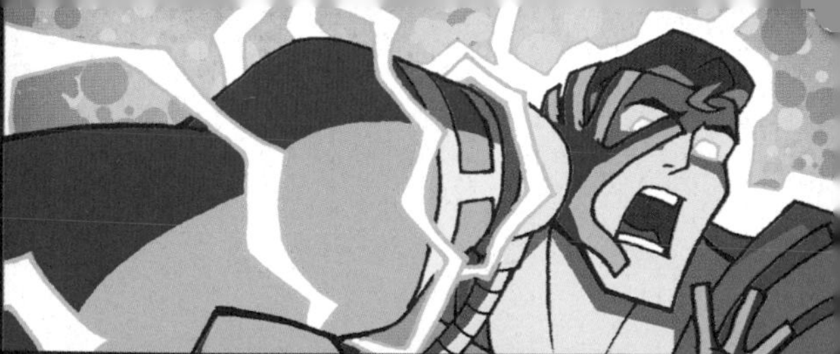
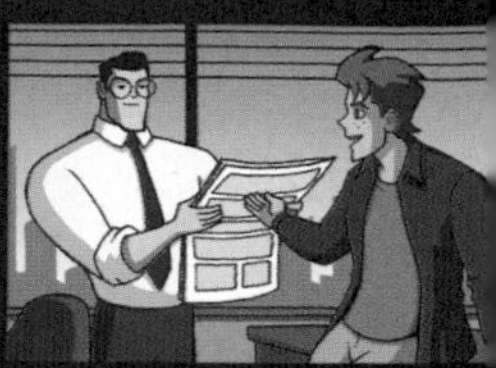

COMIC CHAPTER BOOKS

DC COMICS™ SUPER HEROES

SUPERMAN™

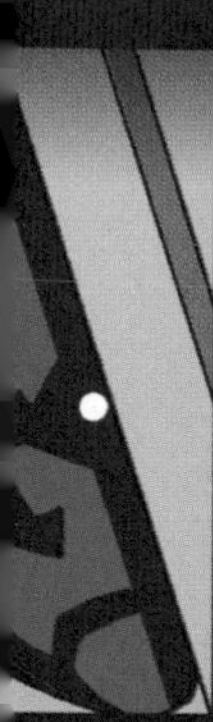
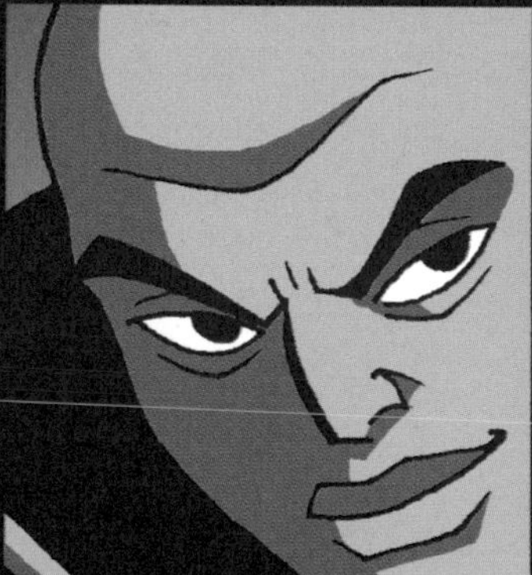

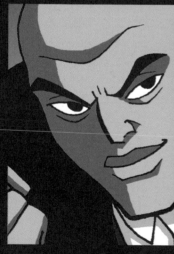

LEX LUTHOR'S POWER GRAB!

written by Louise Simonson

illustrated by Luciano Vecchio

Superman created by Jerry Siegel and Joe Shuster
By special arrangement with the Jerry Siegel family

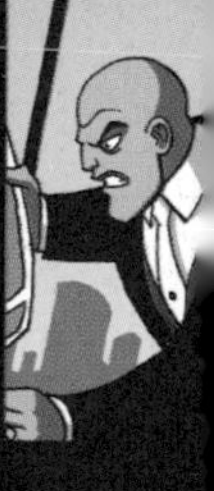
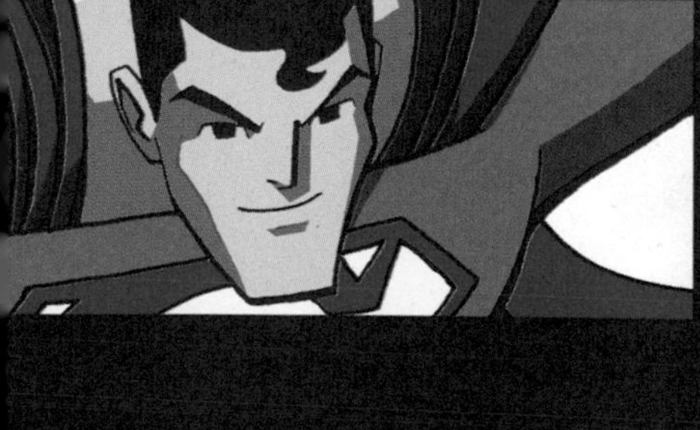
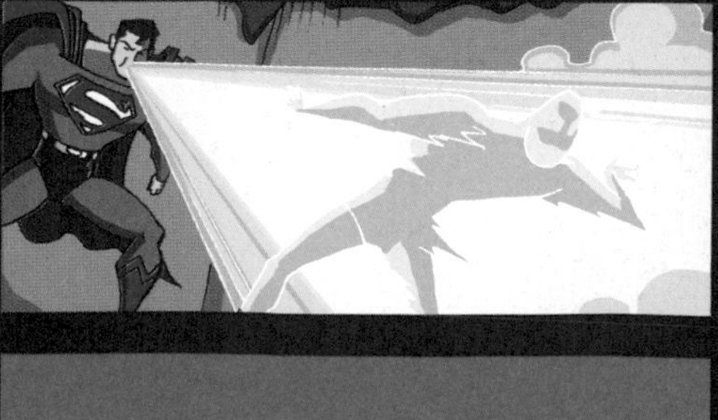

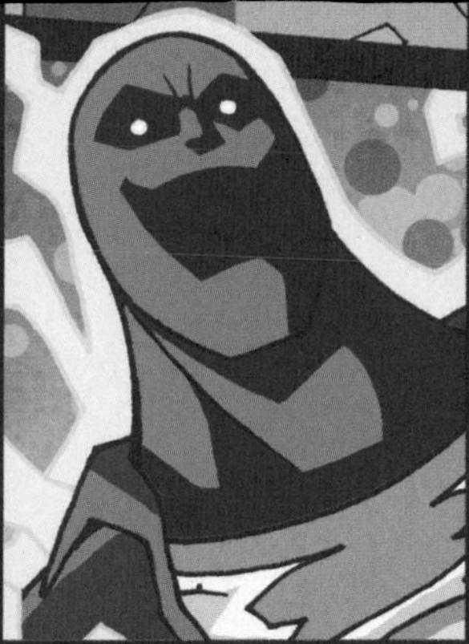

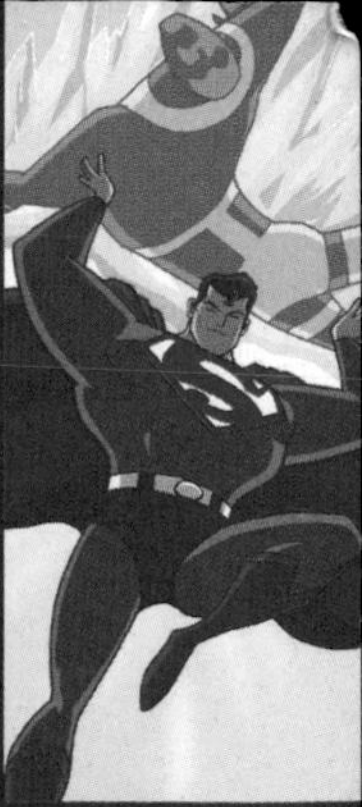

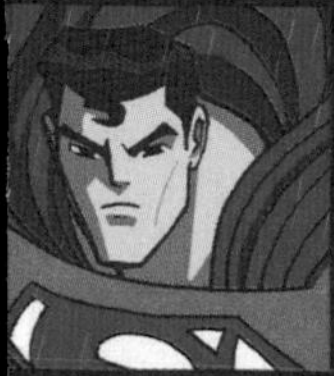

TABLE OF CONTENTS

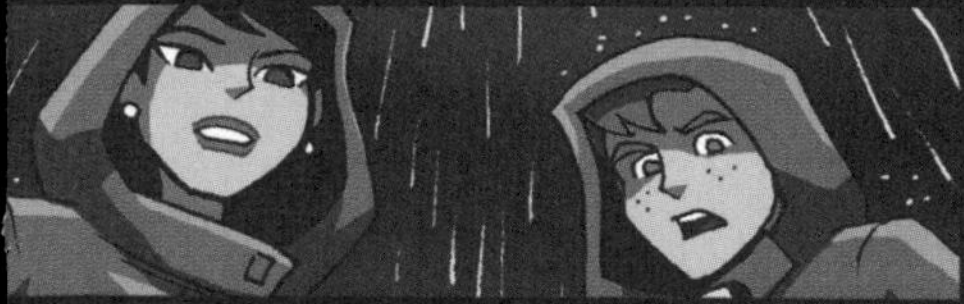

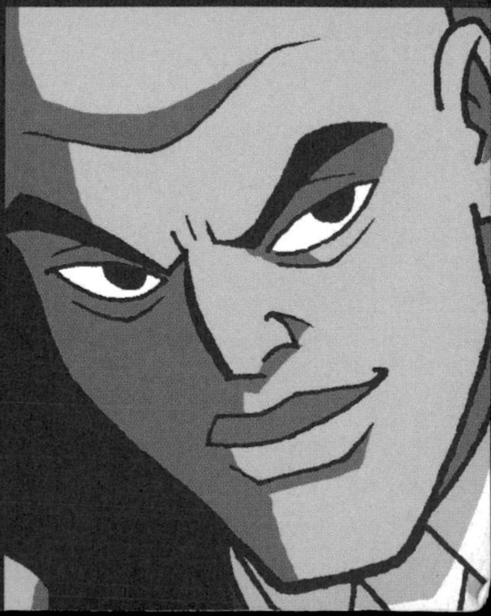

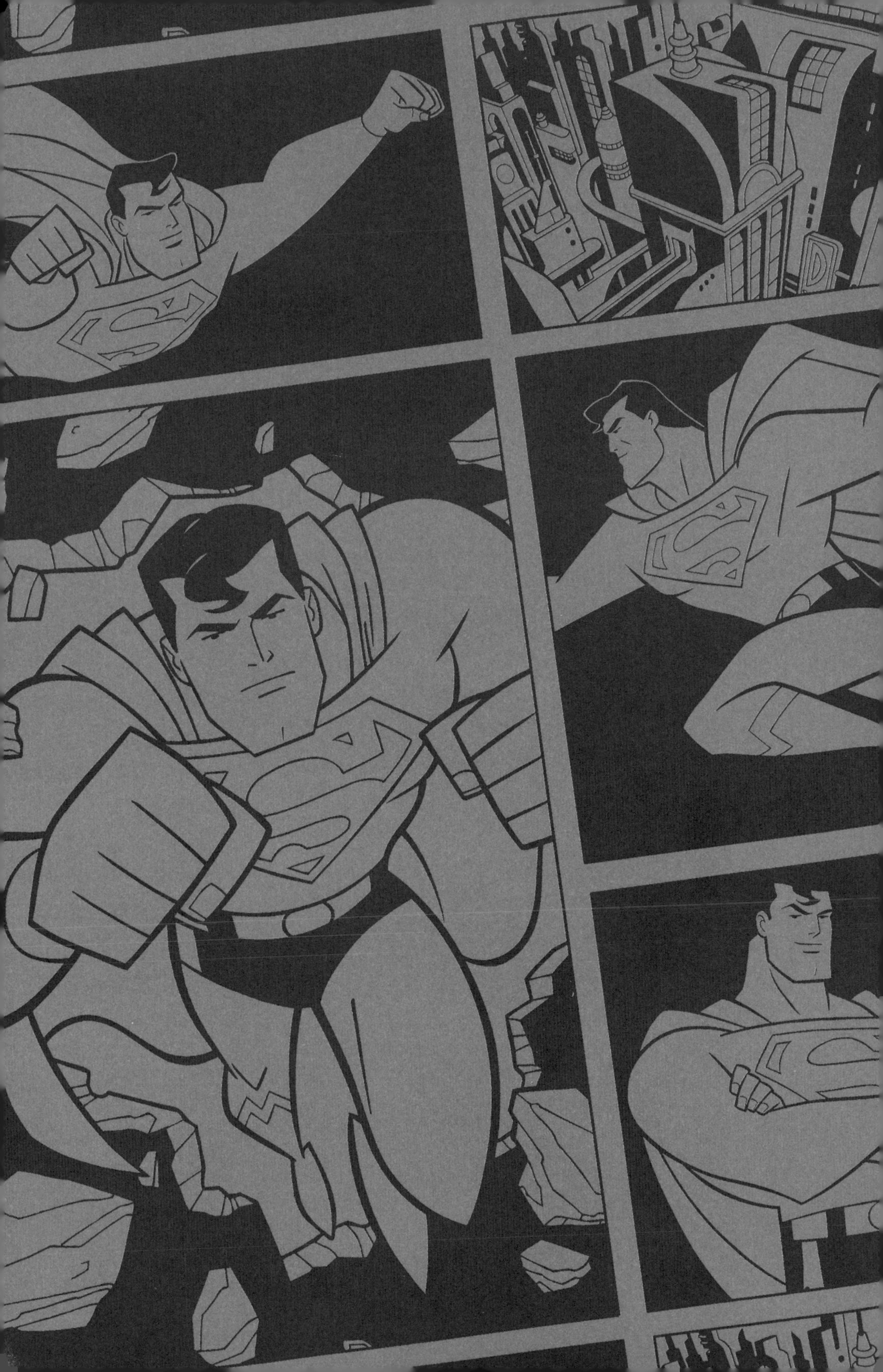

CHAPTER 1

HAMMERZ

High above Metropolis, lightning flashed
as Superman soared through storm clouds.

KRAKA-BOOM!

WOOOOOSH!

WHIP-WHIP-WHIP!

Thunder boomed. Wind buffeted
Superman, sending his cape whipping

behind him. The rain was so heavy it felt like he was swimming through the air.

He scanned the streets below with his X-ray vision. At three in the morning, Metropolis was quiet.

Superman smirked. *It's so wet that even the criminals are staying home,* he thought. *I wish I could go home, too.*

But he couldn't stop patrolling the city. Not with the terrible new energy weapons called Hammerz showing up. They used sound vibration to create incredible force. This force could be fine-tuned to shatter glass or even bring down entire buildings.

When the devices were at full power, Superman felt their blasts despite his invulnerability. He'd seen the Hammerz in the hands of warring gangs as well as in the clutches of thieves. He'd seen the damage they caused. He needed to find their source and stop them from entering his city.

He turned toward the docks. I'll check the waterfront one more time, he thought. *Those force weapons are entering Metropolis somehow.*

Beyond the patter of raindrops, beneath the rumbles of thunder, his super-hearing picked up the sound of a ship's engine as it neared Metropolis harbor.

Not a big ship, he thought. *It sounds more like a yacht. But what's a yacht doing out in this weather?*

* * *

A freak storm had hit Metropolis, but it wouldn't stop *Daily Planet* reporter Lois Lane and photographer Jimmy Olsen from getting their story. They crouched on the roof of a warehouse across from the Metropolis docks, squinting through driving rain. Usually cranes were off-loading the huge cargo ships docked at the wharf. But the area was deserted.

"I guess it's too dangerous to unload cargo tonight," Lois said.

RRRRRRRUMBLE.

"What's that?" Jimmy said.

Lois squinted through binoculars at the single small ship that was pulling up to the pier. "It's a cargo ship," she said. "Called *Destiny*."

"You sure?" Jimmy asked. "It looks more like a big yacht than a cargo ship."

FWOOSH!

A gust of wind blew back the hood of Lois's raincoat. "I think it's a smuggler vessel," she said. "Looks like it's built more for evading the authorities than making large scale deliveries. Plus, it's sneaking in with its lights off. Luthor probably brings in the Hammerz a few crates at a time."

"If the guy behind the Hammerz really is Lex Luthor," Jimmy grumbled, "he couldn't have asked for better cover to off-load his cargo. It may be too dark to get decent photos —"

VRRROOMMMM!

"There!" Lois pointed. An unmarked truck was pulling onto the pier. Lights on the deck of the Destiny flashed on. "Something's happening."

Jimmy pointed his camera at the ship. "That's more like it!" he said, beginning to snap photos.

CLICK CLICK CLICK!

As the truck slowed to a stop, the Destiny lowered a gangplank. Sailors began to move around on the deck.

"Some of them have Hammerz," Jimmy whispered.

"Good," Lois whispered. "Your photos will prove this is part of the illegal weapons smuggling chain."

"Transport's here! Unload the cargo," came a voice from the Destiny. "And be quick about it!"

"Sounds like the guy in charge," Lois said.

SQUEAK! SKREEEE! SPLASH!

A burly sailor began to wheel a dolly carrying a large crate down the gangplank. The truck driver leapt from his cab and splashed through puddles to slide open the rear door.

Lightning revealed a flash of movement just below the clouds. Something was coming, and fast.

KRAKA-BOOM!

Thunder rolled.

"Do you see that?" Lois whispered, shielding her eyes from the blinding light.

"See what?" Jimmy asked.

Aboard the yacht, a sailor was pointing his Hammer skyward to shield his eyes from the rain. "Something's up there!" the man shouted.

The guy beside him snorted. "You're such a coward," he said. "It's just an airplane or something."

"That's no airplane," the captain yelled from up on the bridge. "It's Superman! All hands on deck — get him!"

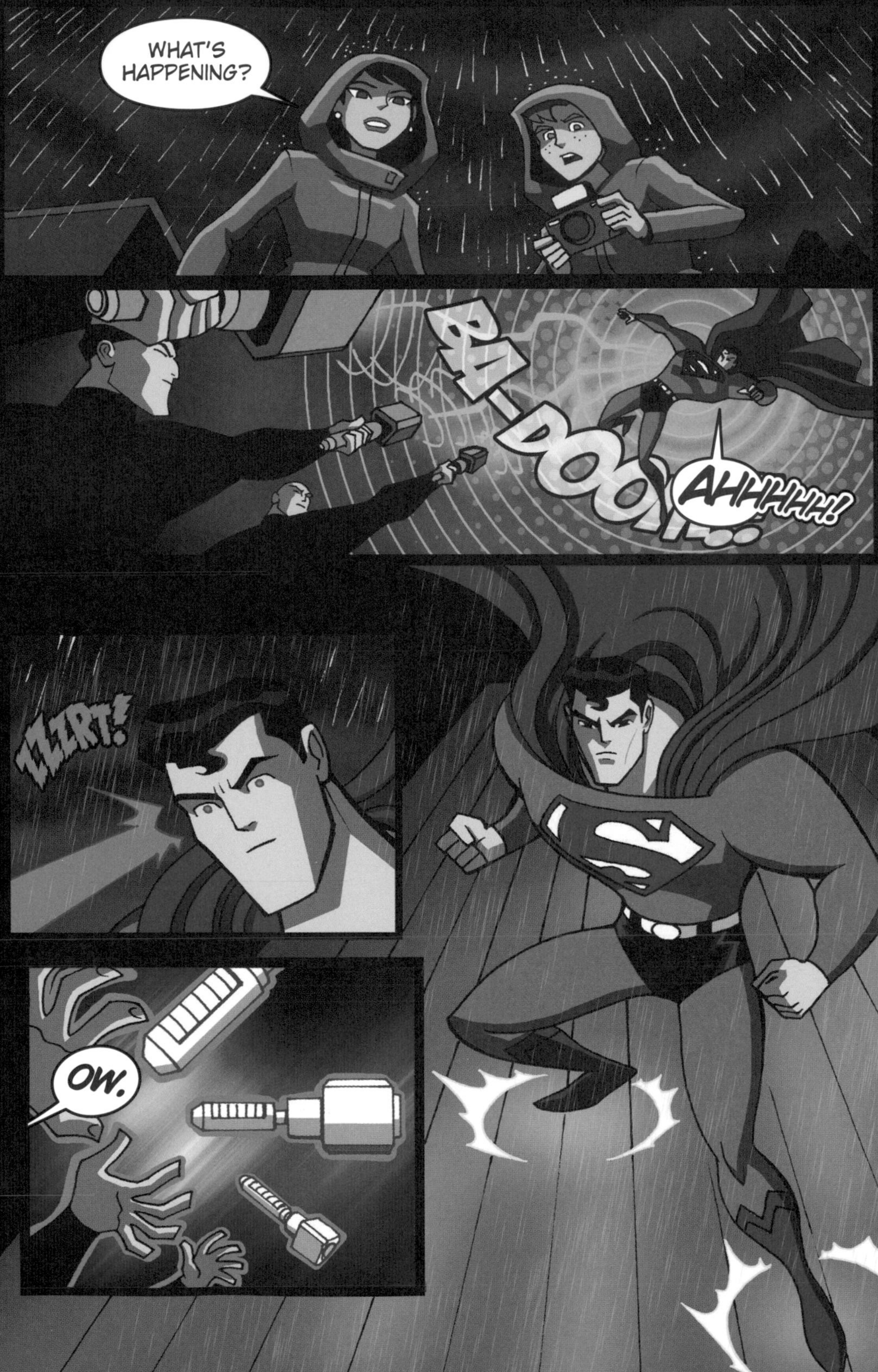
WHAT'S HAPPENING?
BA-DOOM...
AHHHHHH!
ZZZRT!
OW.

Superman scanned the yacht with X-ray vision. Crates filled with Hammerz were piled in the main cabin below.

Out of the corner of his eye, he saw movement up on the bridge. The captain had grabbed another Hammer and was pointing it at Superman. Superman leapt skyward at super-speed.

WHAMMMM!

The force of the blast smashed a hole through the deck where he had been standing and continued into the engine room below.

Before the Captain could fire again, Superman dived from the sky and snatched the weapon from the captain's hand. He bent it in half and tossed it into the ocean.

SPLASH!

Superman frowned. An odd smell was filling the air.

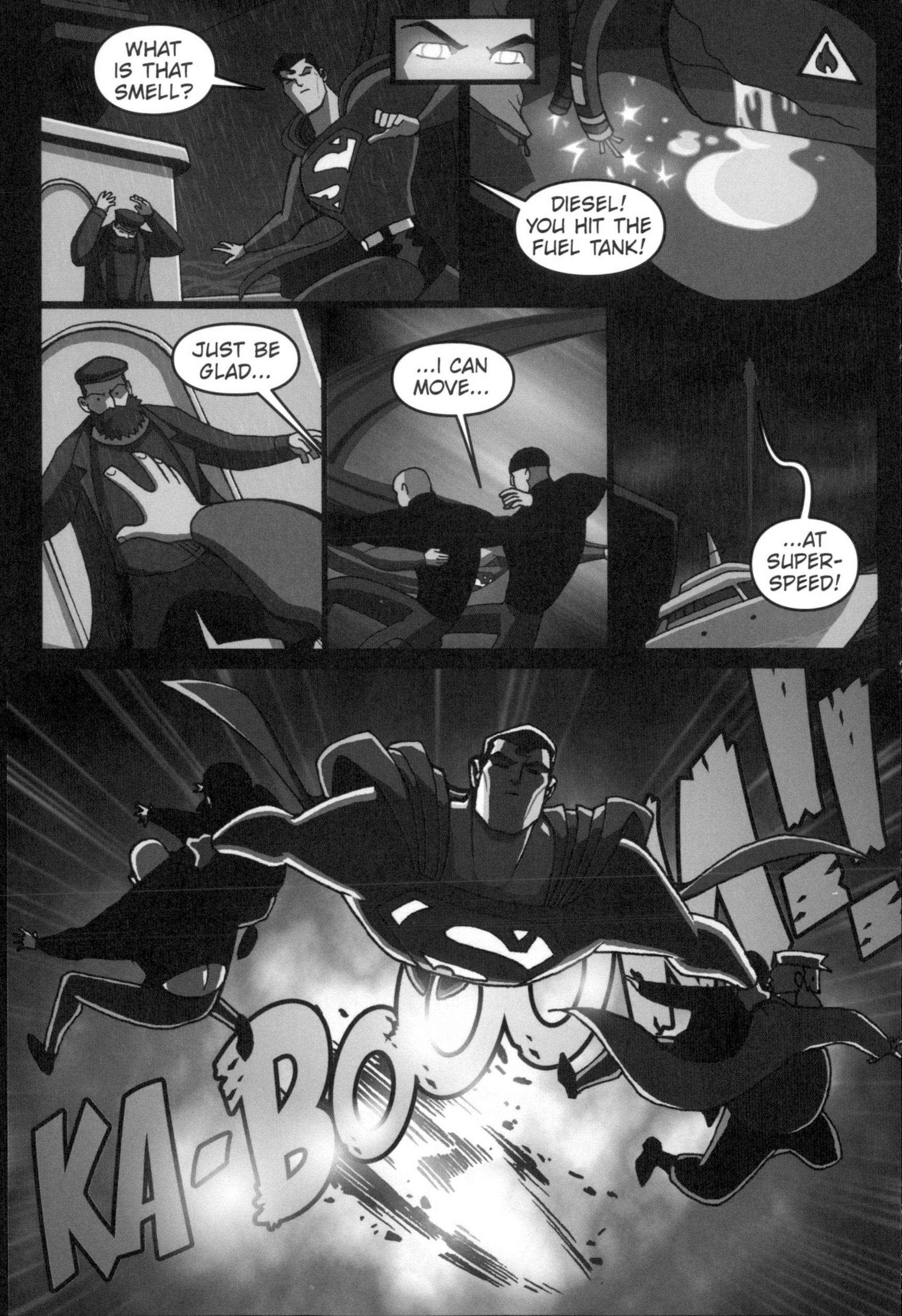

WHAT IS THAT SMELL?
DIESEL! YOU HIT THE FUEL TANK!
JUST BE GLAD...
...I CAN MOVE...
...AT SUPER-SPEED!
KA-BOOM

Superman landed on the pier with the captive smugglers. A smashed box of force weapons lay in a puddle. The truck had sped off the second Superman had appeared.

WHOOP-WHOOP-WHOOP!

He heard police sirens heading this way.

Good, Superman thought. *Let the cops question these smugglers. Not that they would know much. The man behind the scheme was good at keeping secrets.*

Superman sighed. He had stopped one shipment of Hammerz from entering Metropolis. But any evidence aboard the yacht had been destroyed in the explosion.

As cop cars screeched onto the pier, Superman's super-hearing picked up a quiet sound.

CLICK-CLICK-CLICK

Superman recognized that sound. He glanced at the warehouse roof.

CLICK
CLICK
CLICK!

Jimmy Olsen was standing there, snapping photographs. Lois Lane was beside him taking notes. Both of them were doing their jobs despite the pounding rain.

More police were coming. Superman knew other reporters would soon follow. But his friends had been there first, as usual. They'd gotten the real story and had the pictures to prove it.

Superman felt proud of them, but also worried. His two friends would try as hard as he did to find the source of the Hammerz. But they hadn't come from the planet Krypton, like he had. They didn't have superpowers. They weren't invulnerable.

These Hammerz are too dangerous, Superman thought. *Tomorrow, I'll try to talk Lois and Jimmy out of tracking down the smugglers.*

After all, this was a job for Superman alone.

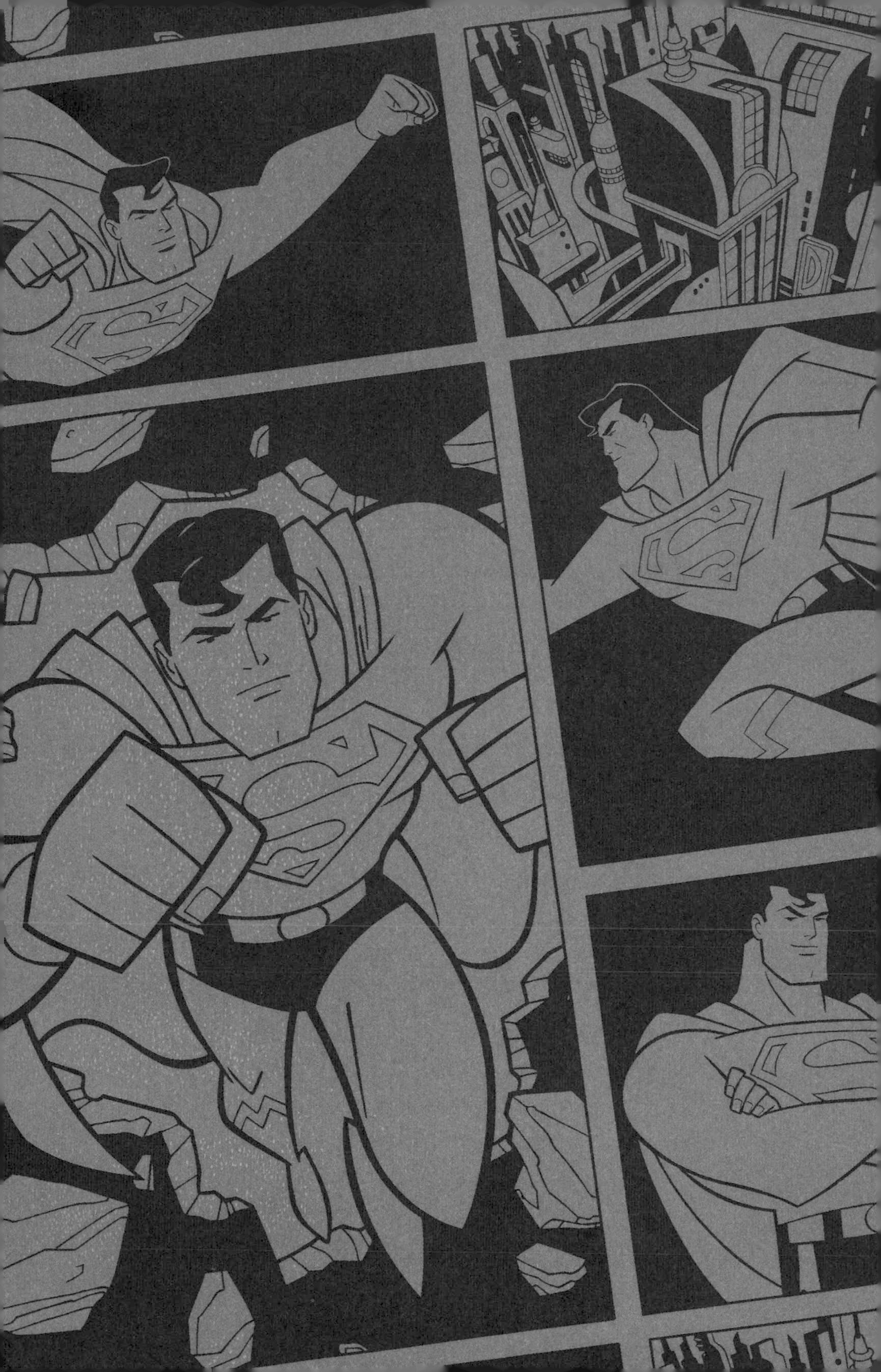

CHAPTER 2

METROPOLIS' FAVORITE HERO

THE NEXT DAY...

Clark ignored the bustle in the *Daily Planet* newsroom as he studied the front page of the newspaper over Lois's shoulder. The headline read: *METROPOLIS' HERO HALTS WEAPONS SMUGGLERS.* There was a large picture of Superman using his heat vision on the Hammerz.

"Looks like you and Jimmy got your story," Clark said.

Lois frowned. "I know. But it isn't the story I wanted. I know Luthor is sneaking those weapons into Metropolis. I just can't prove it. *Yet.*"

Clark shrugged. "But why would Luthor do something like that?" he asked, trying to figure out how to talk Lois into quitting. "And now that Superman has stopped the shipments, it's over."

Lois stuck out her chin. "I don't think so," she said. "I just know Luthor's behind this and I'm not going to stop until I prove it."

Clark knew that expression. There was no stopping Lois on this one. All he could do was warn her.

"I'm sure that you and Jimmy will figure it out," Clark said. "Just be careful."

Lois grinned at him. "I'm always careful."

Now I know I have to keep my eye on her, Clark thought.

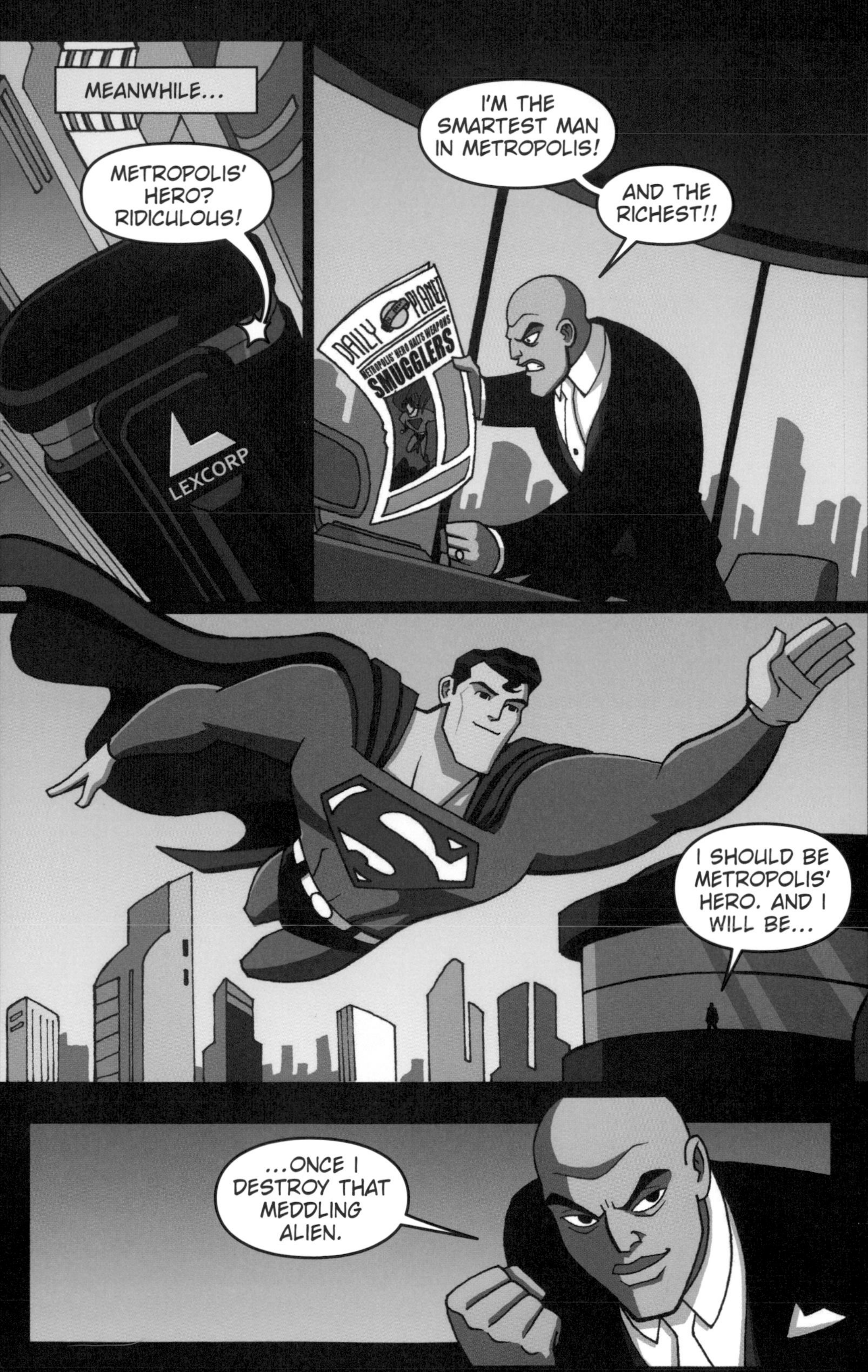
MEANWHILE...
METROPOLIS' HERO? RIDICULOUS!
LEXCORP
I'M THE SMARTEST MAN IN METROPOLIS!
AND THE RICHEST!!
DAILY PLANET
SMUGGLERS
I SHOULD BE METROPOLIS' HERO. AND I WILL BE...
...ONCE I DESTROY THAT MEDDLING ALIEN.

Lex Luthor glanced toward the West River at Stryker's Island. The maximum-security prison there held many of Metropolis' superpowered criminals. He knew that one of the cells held a super-villain called the Parasite.

"That monster can drain Superman's powers," Lex said to himself. "It will be simple to bribe the guards to look the other way. Simpler still to hack into Stryker's computer network and release that monster. The tricky part will be imprisoning him myself." Luthor paced back and forth in front of the window, rubbing his chin. "I'll need to create a distraction for Superman so he can't interfere..."

THREE DAYS LATER...

Parasite sat inside his cell on Stryker's Island behind a wall of bulletproof Plexiglas. It was after midnight, but that didn't matter.

His cell had no window. To him, all time seemed the same.

He was thin and shrunken in his orange prison uniform. His purple skin glowed in the fluorescent light.

He was hungry, but not for food. They gave him plenty of that. He had a taste for a different sort of thing.

He followed the night guards as they opened the shielded exterior door and entered the short hall that faced his private prison. He recognized one of the guards, the old bald one. The younger one was new.

Those guards are walking energy bars to me, he thought. *Dangling just out of my reach. If I could just touch them . . .*

"Ugly fella," the new guard said, staring at Parasite. "What's he in for?"

"You ain't heard of the Parasite?" the bald guard asked.

"That's the Parasite?" the kid said. "I thought the Parasite was this giant, superpowered purple monster."

"Dude's an energy vampire," the older guard said. "He can drain the life from any living thing he touches. He can get some energy from things like batteries, but it's life energy he prefers. Most of all, he wants Superman's energy because he gets some of his superpowers for a while after feeding on him."

Parasite stirred restlessly. He remembered Superman's alien energy all too well. It had been like a drug. An addiction.

The young guard frowned. "He's looking at us like he wants to eat us."

The bald guard shrugged. "Isn't gonna happen. But give him a batch of people to drain and he'll get bigger and uglier and stronger."

He swiped a key card over a scanner. For

a moment, the door into the main corridor slid back open. "It's why he's kept isolated, why everything in his cell is automated. We just have to do a visual check on him every half-hour. That's as close as we ever get to him. It'd be chaos if he got his hands on one of us."

SHWIPPPT!

One of the Plexiglas panels that covered the Parasite's cell slid back into the wall. An exit into the short interior hall had opened.

For a moment, Parasite sat and stared wide-eyed at the open door. Then he lurched to his feet and staggered through the gap.

The guards whirled around and saw Parasite hobbling toward them.

"What the heck?" the young guard said. "He got loose!"

"Close the door!" cried the older guard.

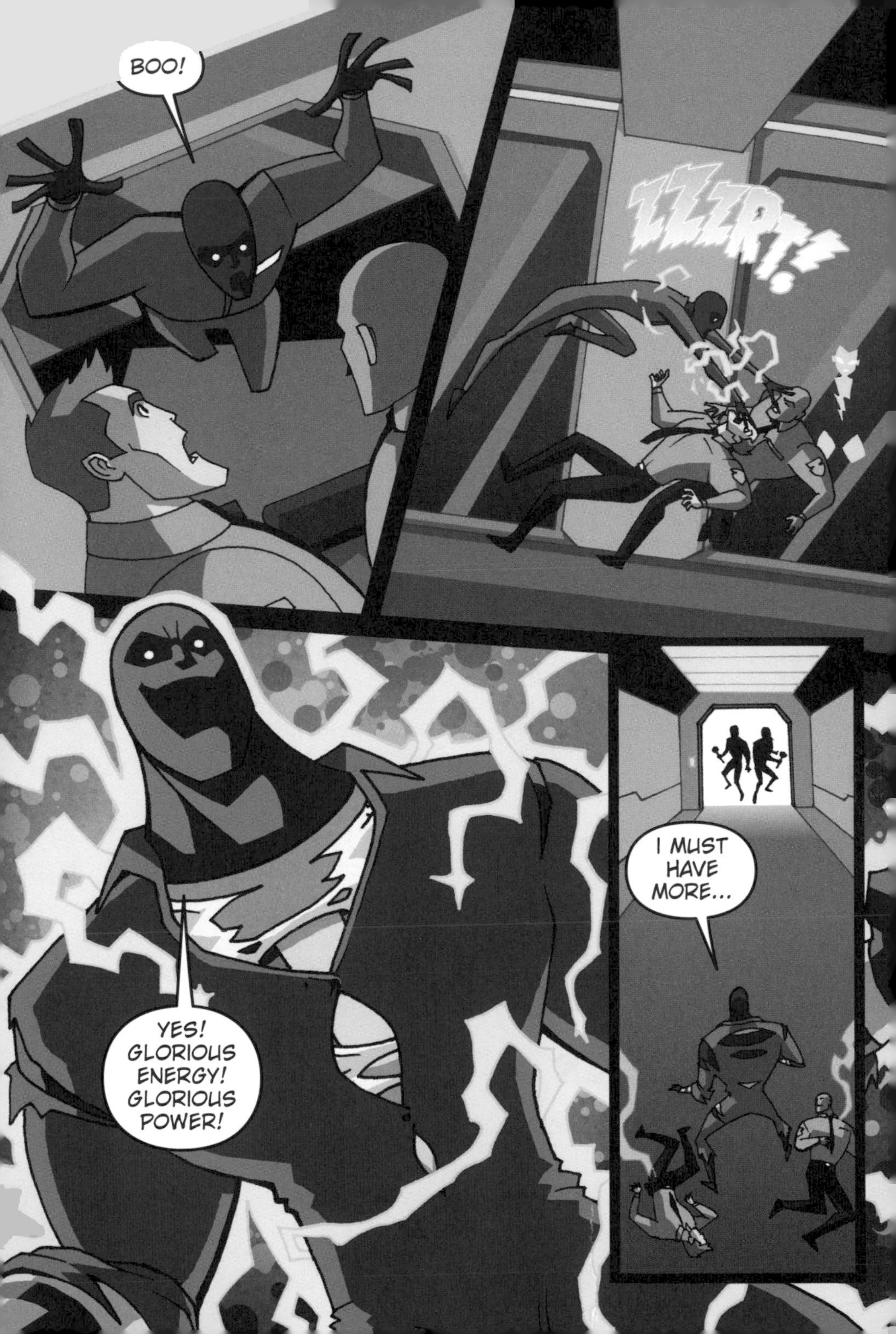
BOO!
ZZZRT!
YES! GLORIOUS ENERGY! GLORIOUS POWER!
I MUST HAVE MORE...

This is too good to be true! Parasite thought. Whatever was happening, he planned to take full advantage of it.

Parasite tossed the guards aside before they were completely drained. Fresher energy was coming his way.

He rushed toward the door at the two men holding Hammerz.

Another snack or two and I'll be ready go after Superman! he thought.

The two men pointed the Hammerz at him.

BA-BOOM!

A force slammed Parasite against the wall. "What's going on?" he cried.

He stood up and dashed at the guards again.

BA-BOOOOM!

This time, the force hit harder. Parasite fell. He was too dizzy to stand up.

"The boss has blocked the security cameras for another five minutes," he heard one of the men say. "We need to get this monster out of here. Use your gloves. Don't touch him. Get these restraints on him and get him on the boat, pronto. The boss wants him off Stryker's Island before the prison officials realize he's missing."

Parasite blacked out.

MEANWHILE...

Superman hovered in the air above Metropolis. At just before midnight, the city seemed peaceful enough.

BA-BOOM!

Was that thunder? Superman thought, glancing up. The sky was clear.

He listened with his super-hearing.

BRRRING!
BRRRING!
BRRRING!

A burglar alarm was ringing.

WHOOP-WHOOP-WHOOP!

A cop car's siren added to the noise.

Superman searched the streets with his super-vision.

An alarm was going off at a jewelry store. Its front door and window had been shattered. Lights in the apartments above it flashed on.

FWOOOOOOSH!

Superman dived toward the store. He scanned the scene with his X-ray vision. He immediately noticed a few things.

The glass jewelry cases had been shattered and were empty.

Two masked men were running toward the back of the store.

One man was pulling a heavy duffel bag behind him. The other man held one of the Hammerz.

Superman landed next to a police car that was parked halfway on the curb. Two cops were racing into the building.

"This is the police!" they yelled. "Come out with your hands up!"

"Wait!" Superman shouted. "Don't go in there. It isn't safe!"

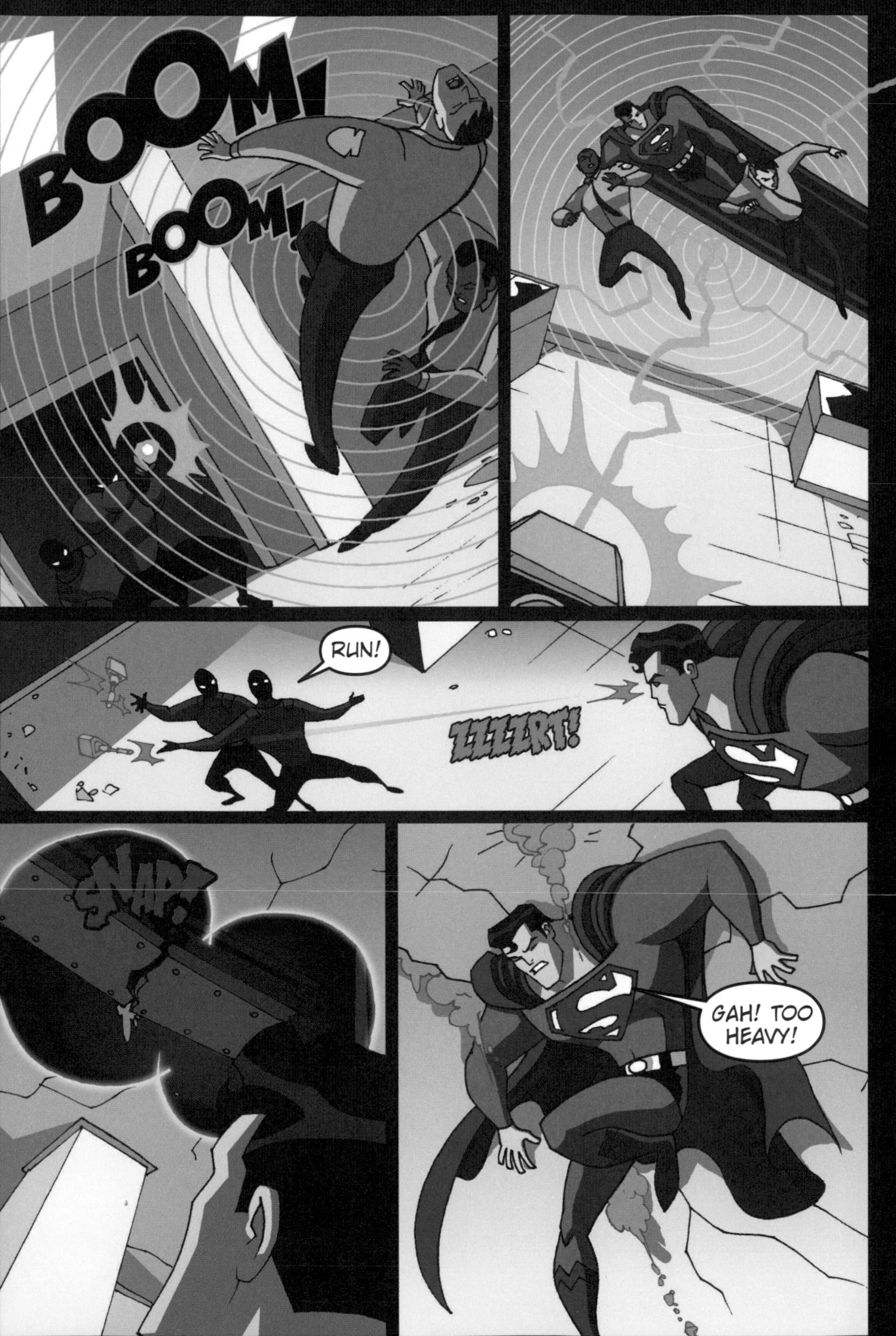
BOOM!
BOOM!
RUN!
ZZZZRT!
SNAP!
GAH! TOO HEAVY!

The cops got to their feet. "We . . . we're okay," one said. "How can we help you, Superman?"

"Evacuate the apartments upstairs! Hurry!" Superman shouted. "I'll prevent the building from collapsing until everyone is safe outside."

The policemen turned and rushed up the steps. They knocked on doors and yelled at the tenants to get out as quickly as they could.

Superman hovered in the air amid crumbling plaster and dust. The burglar alarm was still ringing. The robbers had gotten away, but thankfully they had left their dangerous weapons behind, and no one had gotten hurt.

REEE-OOOO!
REEE-OOOO!

Superman heard sirens. More police were coming. He knew that reporters would soon follow. His friends, Lois Lane and Jimmy Olsen, would be among them.

Thankfully the danger was over. No need to worry — this time.

BA-BOOM!
BA-BOOM!

Superman's super-hearing picked up the faint sound of Hammerz blasting in the distance. He wanted to rush to the scene, but he had to continue to brace the building for a few moments longer.

I have a lot of superpowers, but I don't have eyes in the back of my head, he thought. *Just as well. That would make it harder to keep my identity a secret.*

Moments later, amid the roar of police cars and fire engines, Superman heard the distant blare of security alarms on Stryker's Island.

That had to mean there'd been a jailbreak or someone escaped. But there was nothing he could do about it now.

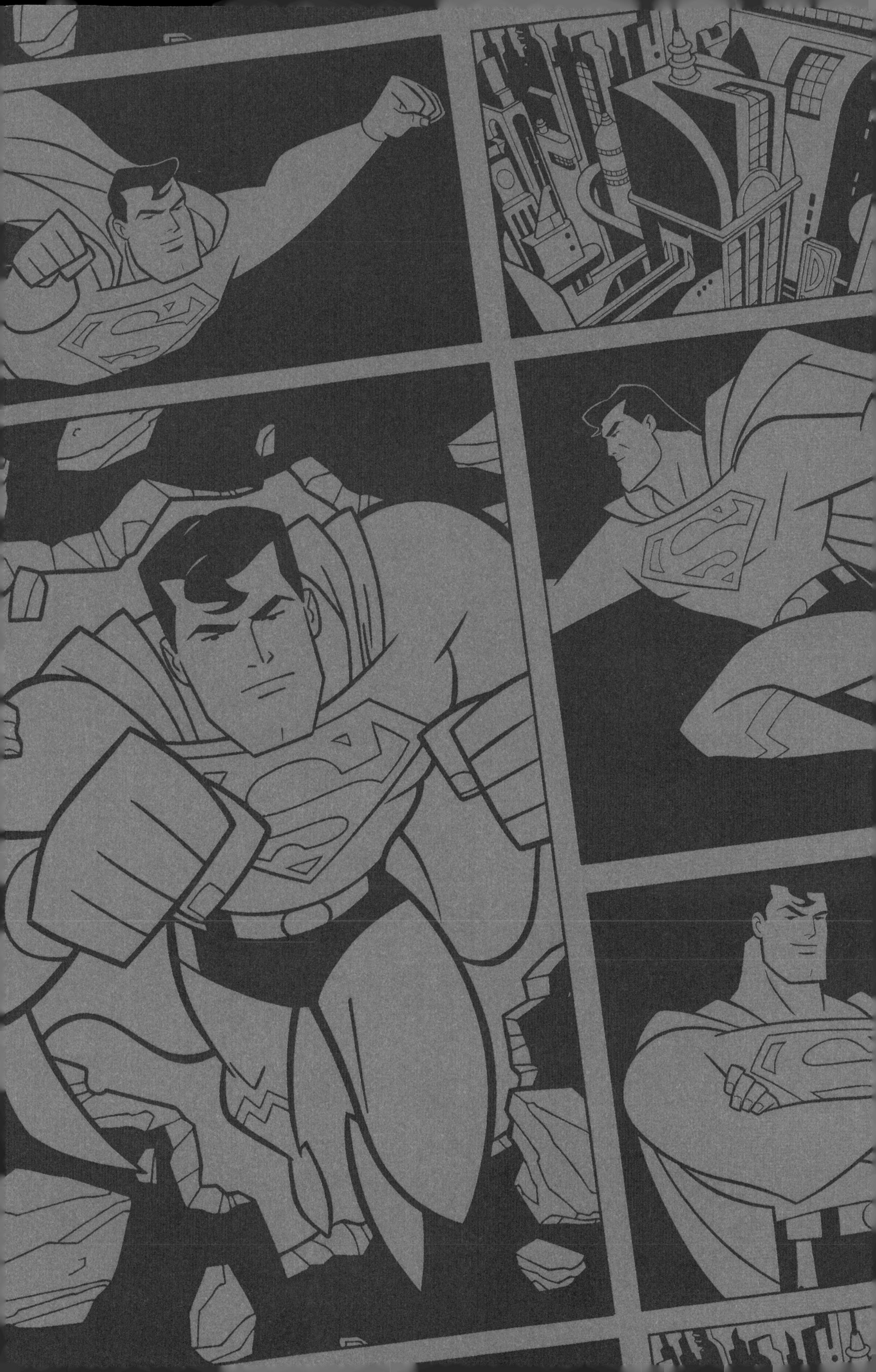

CHAPTER 3

THE TRAP

Parasite awoke in a strange rectangular chamber. Metal rings were around his neck and wrists. Thick chains ran from them to massive brackets in the wall behind him.

KLANK! KLANK!

His muscles bulged through the rips in his orange jumpsuit as he tried to pull them free. But the chains wouldn't budge.

Parasite spotted a masked man. He was studying the villain critically, standing just beyond his reach.

"I have a proposal," the masked man said. "Are you ready to listen?"

Parasite roared in fury and frustration.

KLANK! KLINK! KLUNK!

He wrenched at his chains, frantic to get his hands on his new jailor and steal his life force.

Luthor watched in fascination as the captive Parasite lost more and more energy as he continued to struggle. Slowly Parasite shrank from a purple giant to a slender man.

But as Parasite shriveled, his collar and cuffs contracted to remain tight.

Luthor smirked. "Good thing I made those

restraints flexible," he said. "Otherwise you'd have your paws all over me by now."

Parasite hung his head and collapsed to the floor of the chamber. Once again he was the withered being he'd been back on Stryker's Island.

"About my proposal," Luthor said. "Are you ready to listen now?"

Parasite didn't bother to glance up at him, but he nodded.

"It involves Superman," Luthor said. "I understand you crave his alien energy more than anything. I can deliver him to you on a silver platter."

Parasite raised his head slowly. "How?" he asked. His voice was as raspy as a creaky hinge.

Luthor rubbed his chin through his mask. "Attracting him won't be difficult," he said. "You will be allowed to drain him for an instant, but that should assuage your hunger

temporarily. After that, you will be allowed
to siphon off his energy at regular intervals
so that he remains in a weakened state."

"What do you get out of it?" Parasite
croaked.

"Superman is powered by the sun's
energy," Luthor said. "I will keep him away
from the sunlight that fuels him until
you're ready to feed on him. Once you have
absorbed his powers, you will use them in
my service. In other words, I will give you
Superman . . . and you will work for me."

Parasite eyes met with Luthor's. "I'll do
it," he croaked.

SEVERAL DAYS LATER...

42

Superman flew over Metropolis harbor. The waning moon shed little light on the container ships docked below.

The dark didn't bother Superman. He used his X-ray vision to search the ships' holds as he flew overhead. He kept hoping to spot another smuggler ship carrying more of the Hammerz. But so far there'd been nothing.

Then, on the deck of an almost empty container ship, he noticed something odd. This time, it wasn't what he saw that bothered him. It was what he couldn't see. His X-ray vision could see through any substance but one: lead. And there, on the deck below, was a container he could not see inside.

Now Superman knew that whoever was importing the Hammerz knew about his odd weakness. It meant someone had something to hide from the Man of Steel.

Superman hesitated to fly down to the deck. *It's like a flashing beacon for me,*

Superman thought. *Don't they think that it'll make me suspicious? It could be a trap . . .*

A quick survey of the area showed the coast was clear. Still, Superman proceeded with caution as he descended on the ship. A guard holding a Hammer stepped out from behind the lead container.

BADOOM!

He fired a pulse, but Superman dodged it at super-speed. He landed and snatched the weapon from the guard.

CRUNCH!

He crushed it with his bare hands.

"Where did you get this?" he asked.

"Um," the guard mumbled. He glanced over at the lead-lined shipping container, which was enough of an answer for Superman.

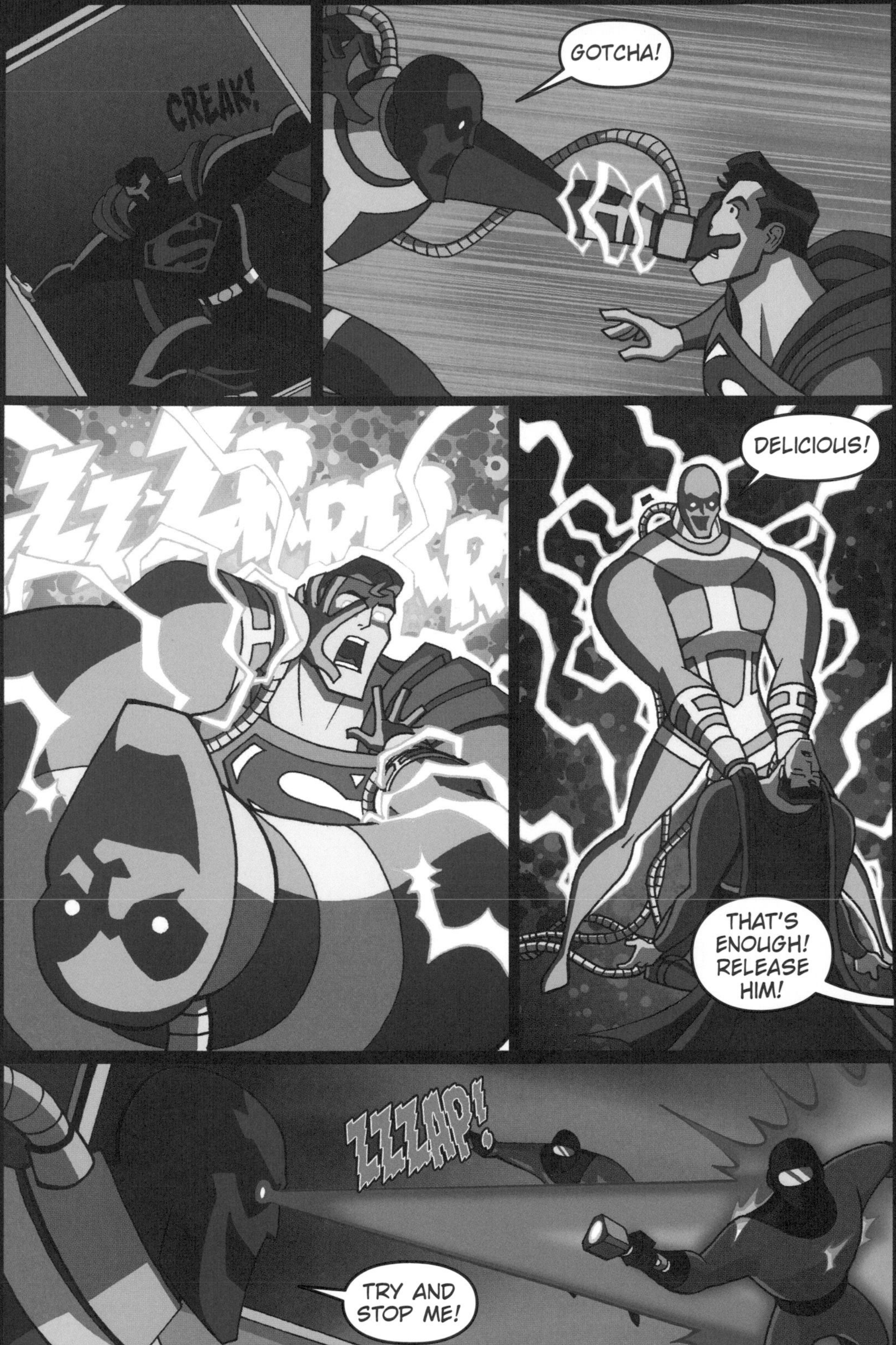
CREAK!
GOTCHA!
DELICIOUS!
THAT'S ENOUGH! RELEASE HIM!
ZZZAP!
TRY AND STOP ME!

Drained and weakened in the monster's grasp, Superman hadn't noticed the guards wearing protective gear at the far end of the container.

BADOOM!
BADOOM!

The guards fired their Hammerz at maximum force. The pulses slammed into Parasite and Superman. Parasite flew backward and Superman was released.

BOOM!
THUD!

The monster and the hero slammed against the container wall, then crashed into a heap on the floor.

Superman struggled to his feet. He had walked into a trap. "You won't get away with this," he said.

A masked man stepped out from the

shadows. "I already have," he said. "Shorten the Parasite's chain — now!" he ordered the guards.

The hum of machinery and grinding of gears rang out. Parasite was dragged into an upright position.

"You see how it works, Parasite?" the masked man said. "Superman is now too weak to resist my weapons, and you did not grow strong enough to withstand them. You are now both my prisoners."

The masked man turned to the guards. "Chain Superman in the cell at the far end of the container," he said. Then he left the container.

Beneath his mask, Luthor felt particularly pleased with himself as he led his guards out the door. Parasite was addicted to Superman's energy and would do whatever Lex asked to get more of it. Since he now controlled Parasite, he also controlled

Superman. Both hero and monster were under his thumb.

Eventually, Lex might let the monster drain all of Superman's energy. But for now, he would use him as a living battery.

"Prepare the container for transport," Lex Luthor said.

CLANG!

The door slammed shut, sealing Parasite and Superman in total darkness.

Superman struggled to stay upright in his cell as the lead-lined container shifted and swayed. He realized it was being lifted off the ship by one of the giant cranes.

THUD!

It landed on a hard surface.

BANG!

He was nearly knocked over as it began to move.

"Where are we going?" Parasite asked.

"Our prison has been loaded onto a flatbed," Superman said. "And a truck is taking us away."

But where? Superman wondered.

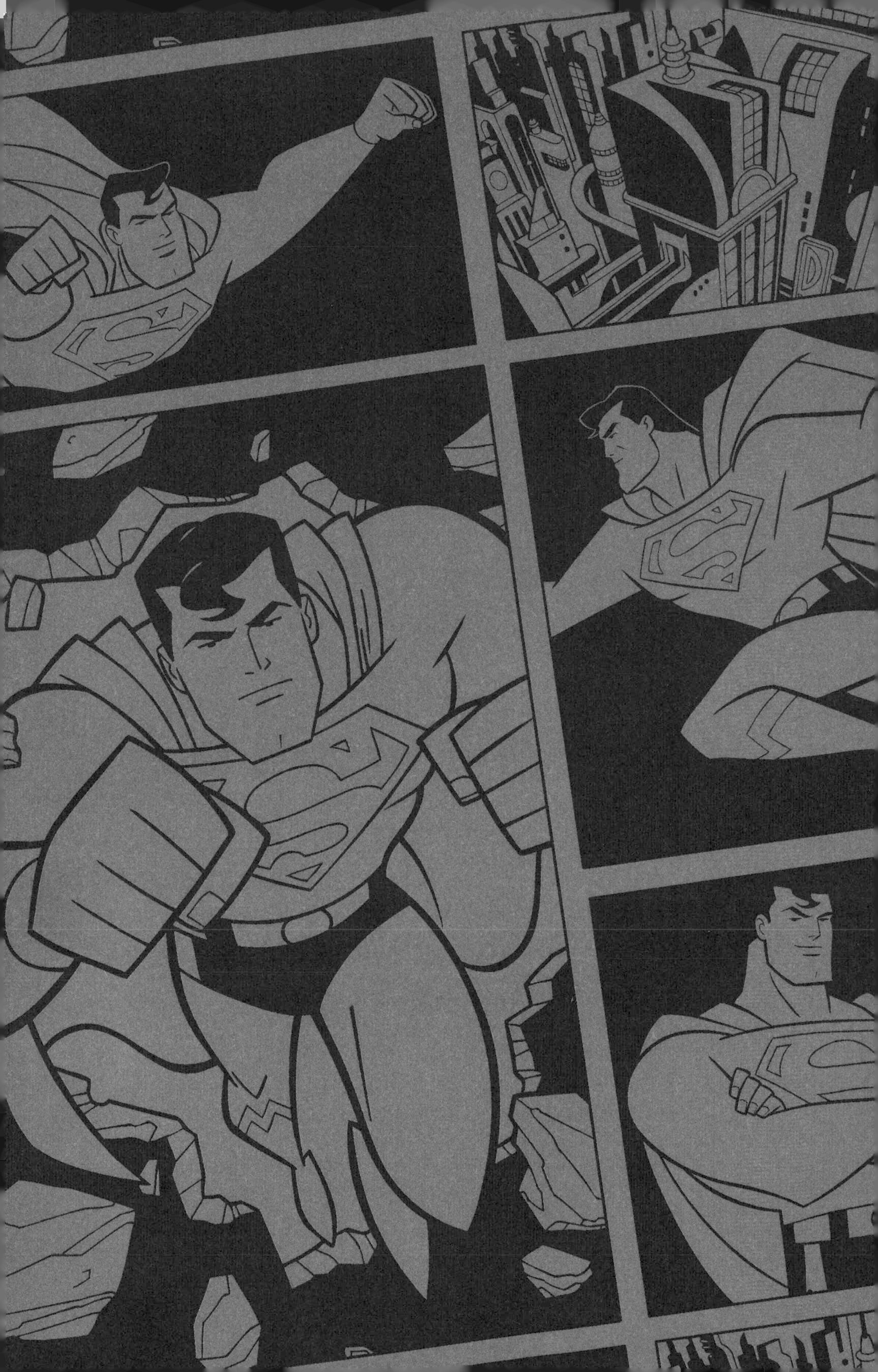

CHAPTER 4

WHERE IS SUPERMAN?

TWO DAYS LATER...

Lois Lane sat across a tree-lined street in Hob's Bay and frowned. There was an ugly, rubble-filled gap where, until that day, a building had stood.

"My favorite coffee shop was here," Lois muttered. "Last week, Superman kept a building just like this from collapsing. Where was he when this one fell?"

She looked around for Jimmy Olsen, but he had wandered down to the crosswalk to take more pictures.

An old woman stomped up to Lois. "You're that reporter!" she said. "You tell your readers it's that Lex Luthor who did this! He wants to knock down these two blocks and put up a high-rise building. But some of us owners don't want to sell! He's trying to force us — !"

BEEP! HONK! BEEP-BEEP!

At the intersection, horns blared as a large container truck lumbered past.

Lois whirled around, startled by the strange noise. Flames were leaping out of the first floor of the corner building. Jimmy was there, first on the scene, taking pictures.

"Probably a gas explosion," Lois said. She pulled out her phone and dialed 911.

"It's that Lex Luthor!" the old woman snarled. "He's behind this, too!"

Yes, Lois thought. *It probably is Luthor. But how did he do it? And where is Superman?*

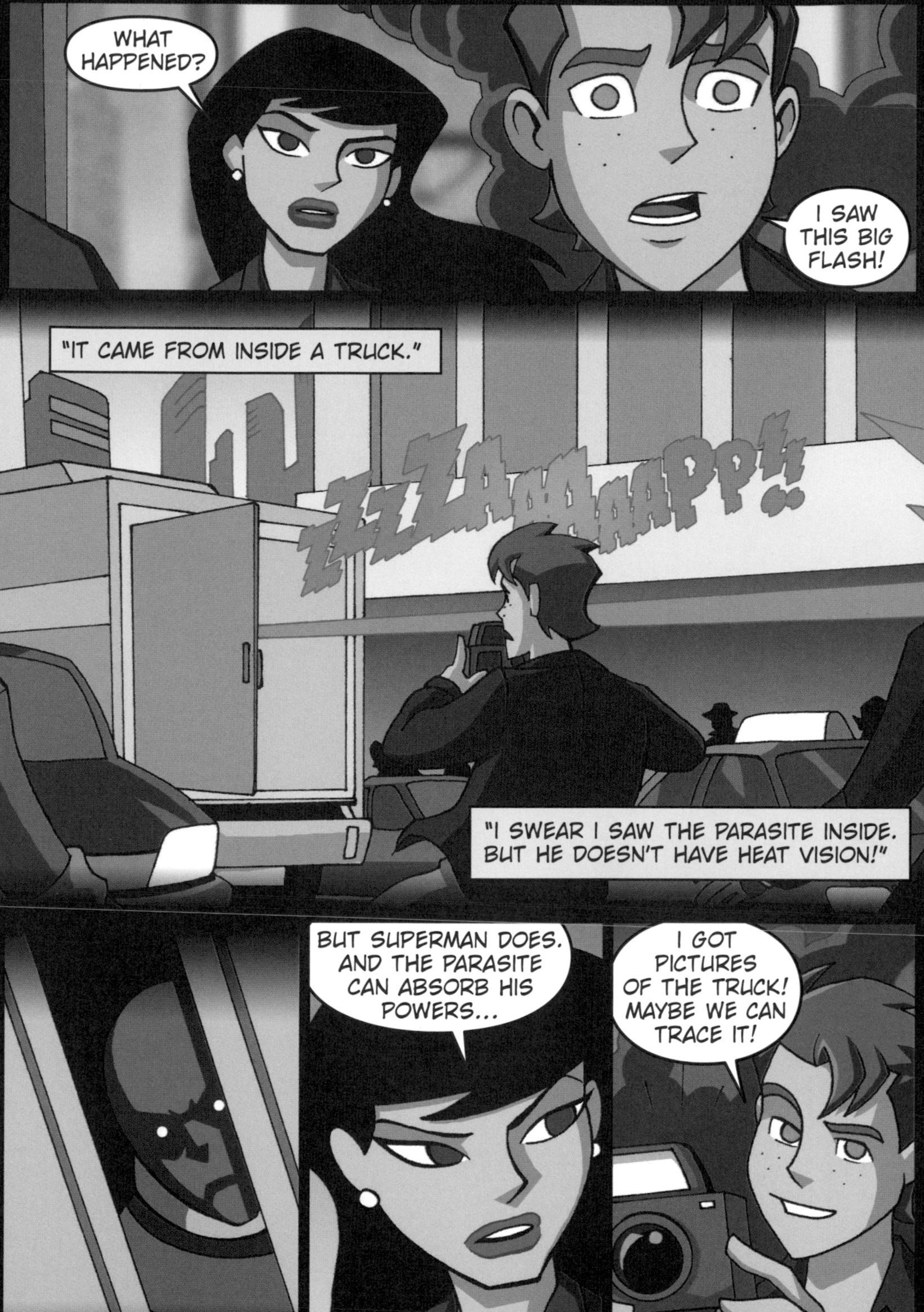
WHAT HAPPENED?
I SAW THIS BIG FLASH!
"IT CAME FROM INSIDE A TRUCK."
ZZZZAAAAAAPP!!
"I SWEAR I SAW THE PARASITE INSIDE. BUT HE DOESN'T HAVE HEAT VISION!"
BUT SUPERMAN DOES. AND THE PARASITE CAN ABSORB HIS POWERS...
I GOT PICTURES OF THE TRUCK! MAYBE WE CAN TRACE IT!

MEANWHILE, BEHIND A NEARBY TRUCK...

Superman lay on his back, staring up toward the roof of his cell, waiting for his captors to leave. He knew he looked weaker than ever, but he was actually stronger. When they had cracked open the door so Parasite could fire his heat vision, a shaft of sunlight had touched his leg.

His superpowers weren't entirely restored, but if his chains were loose enough he might be able to reach the ceiling. He'd spotted a frame that might be a skylight. If it was, and he could open it, sunlight would pour in and he would be able to break free.

KLANG!

His captors left, slamming and locking the doors behind them.

He staggered to his feet in the darkness. Feeling his way, he grabbed the bars to his cage, and, slowly, painfully, he began to climb.

He had made it halfway up when his chains caught. He couldn't reach the skylight with his hands. Maybe he could kick it. If he had enough energy left to try . . .

AT THE SAME TIME...

"That's the right license plate!" Jimmy said. The truck he had photographed was backed up to a crumbling loading dock behind a rundown warehouse. A shiny chain-link fence topped with barbed wire surrounded the place.

Lois crouched beside him. "This fence is new," she said. "Somebody doesn't want visitors. Good thing I came prepared."

"Does Luthor own this place?" Jimmy asked.

"No," Lois said. "But LexCorp owns a firm that has a controlling interest in a company that leases this warehouse. The truck lists that firm as the owner."

"It looks like nobody's home at the moment," Jimmy said.

"Good," Lois said. "Because I want to sneak a look inside that shipping container over there."

Lois positioned her bolt cutters on a fence link. She squeezed the arms together.

SNIP!

Lois kept at it.

**SNIP! SNIP! SNIP!
SNIP! SNIP! SNIP!**

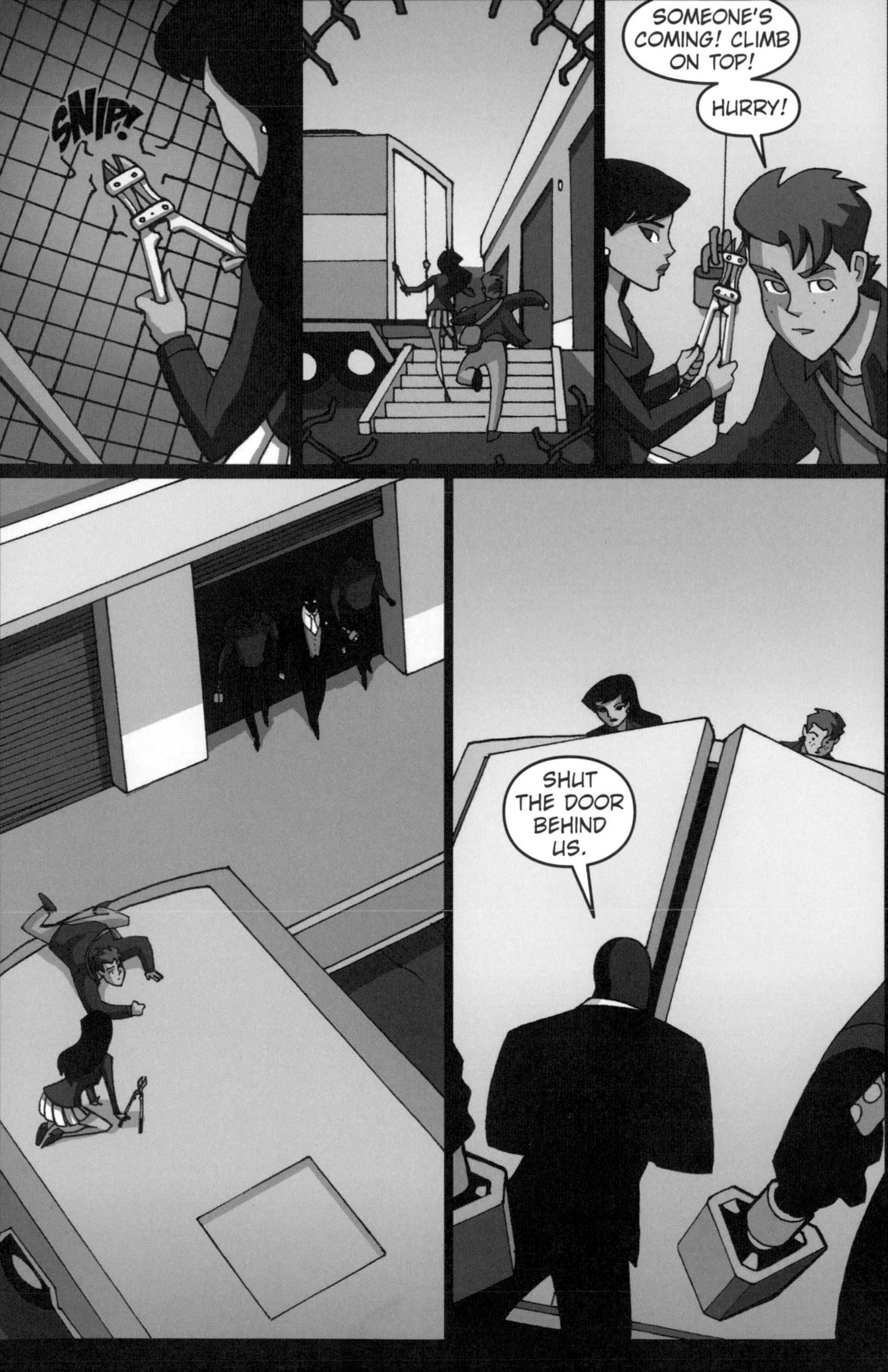
SNIP!
SOMEONE'S COMING! CLIMB ON TOP!
HURRY!
SHUT THE DOOR BEHIND US.

Superman was sweating from his efforts.
One of his kicks had reached the ceiling,
but he had no way of knowing how near he
had been to the skylight, or if it even was a
skylight.

SHHHSSSSSSSS!

He heard a sliding noise on the roof. The
doors to his prison opened, then closed.

CLICK!

The masked leader switched on the
interior light. Now Superman knew where to
aim his kick . . .

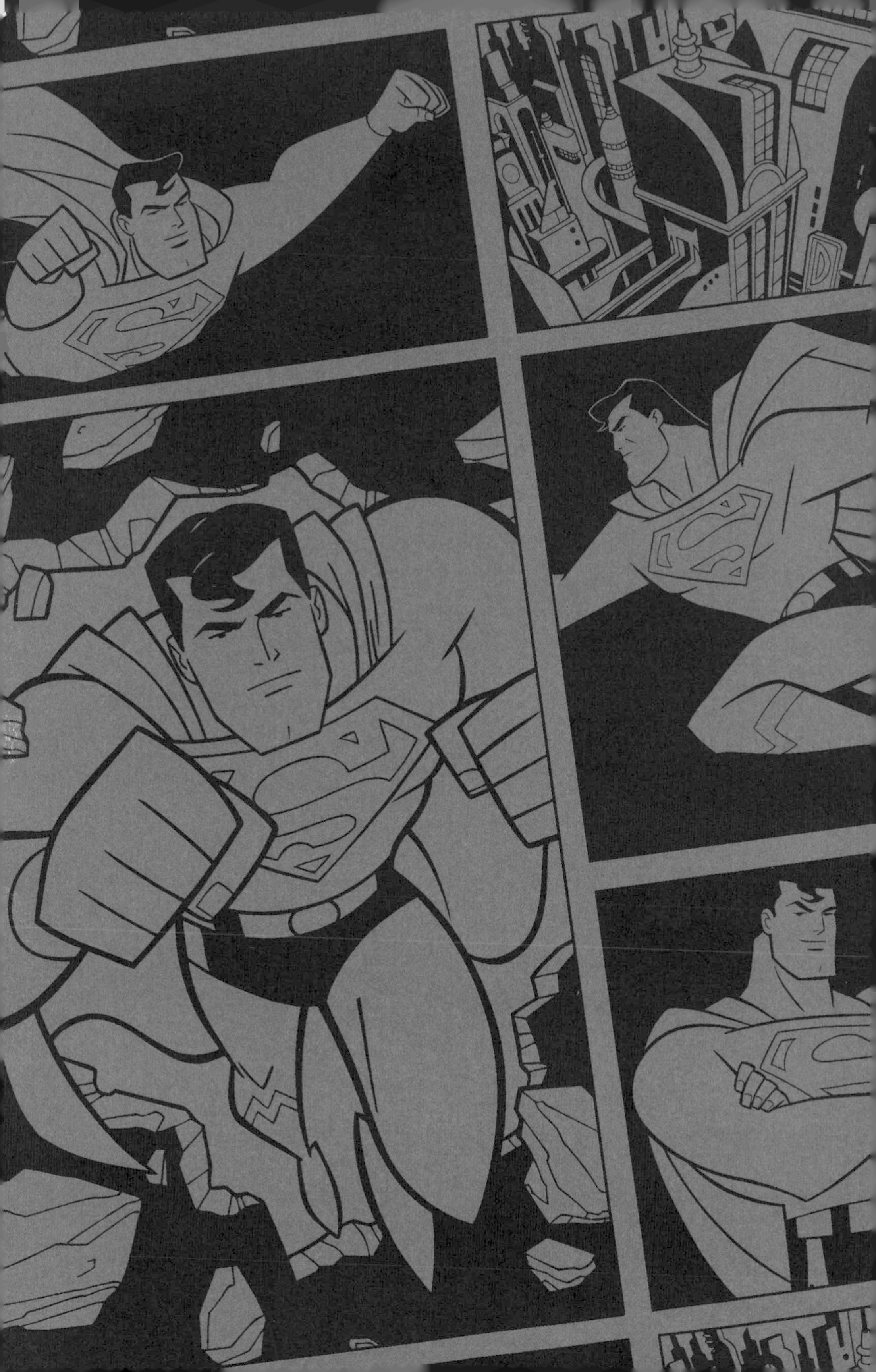

CHAPTER 5

VICTORY

Parasite slumped, trying to look helpless in his orange rags. Superman could tell he was trying to trick their masked captor into giving him another taste of Superman's energy. Parasite was smaller and weaker than he had been, but he was nowhere near the shrunken shell he'd been in prison.

"You promised if I used my remaining power to set that fire, I could drain Superman some more," Parasite croaked.

"And I keep my promises," the masked man said.

KLANG!
KLANG!
KLANG!

He looked over at Superman and chuckled. Superman was up on his bars like a monkey, desperately trying to kick open the skylight. "Put some slack in Parasite's chains," he told the guards. "Let the monster get close enough to touch Superman."

RATTLE-RATTLE!

The chain began to lengthen. As the Parasite staggered toward Superman, the masked man pointed a remote control at the ceiling.

ZMMMMMMMMMM!

A skylight above Superman's cell began to slide open.

Superman, shackled and drained, stared through a widening crack into the noonday sun.

"When sunlight strikes Superman, he will begin to regain his power," the masked man said. "You have three seconds to drain him before I close the skylight and we pull you back. If you retain his power, and disperse it as I tell you, next time I will let you absorb even more."

ON TOP OF THE SAME CONTAINER...

REEEEE!

Lois jerked back as a motorized skylight slid open beneath her. She had been lying on top of it and hadn't even realized it was there.

Sunlight poured in through the opening, illuminating the interior. She peeked over its rim. For a second, she was staring into Superman's face. He was a shell of his former self, but he was alive.

In the light of the sun, he seemed to grow stronger . . .

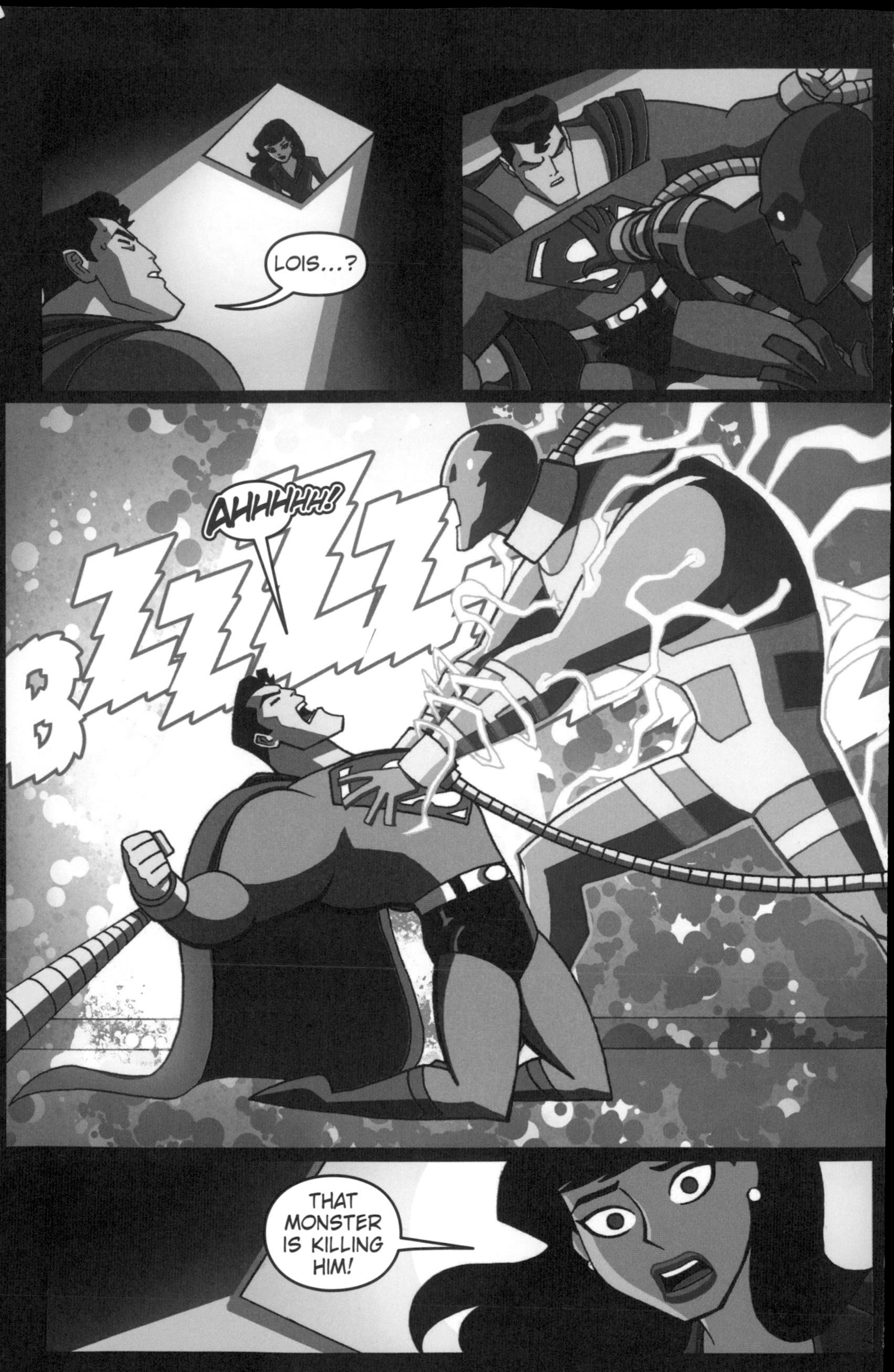
LOIS...?
AHHHHH!
BZZZZZ
THAT MONSTER IS KILLING HIM!

"That's enough!" the masked man shouted. He clicked the remote control. The skylight began to slowly slide shut.

"No!" Parasite roared.

"Tighten Parasite's chains," the masked man ordered. "Hit him with the Hammerz!"

With a powerful tug, the monster ripped his chains from the wall.

FROM ABOVE...

SLAP! WHAP!

Lois watched as Parasite used the broken chains like whips to knock the guards aside. He dropped Superman and lurched toward his masked captor.

Lois was afraid that Superman was dead. When he moved, Lois sighed with relief. Sunlight had, once again, begun to revive him. But the skylight was almost completely closed.

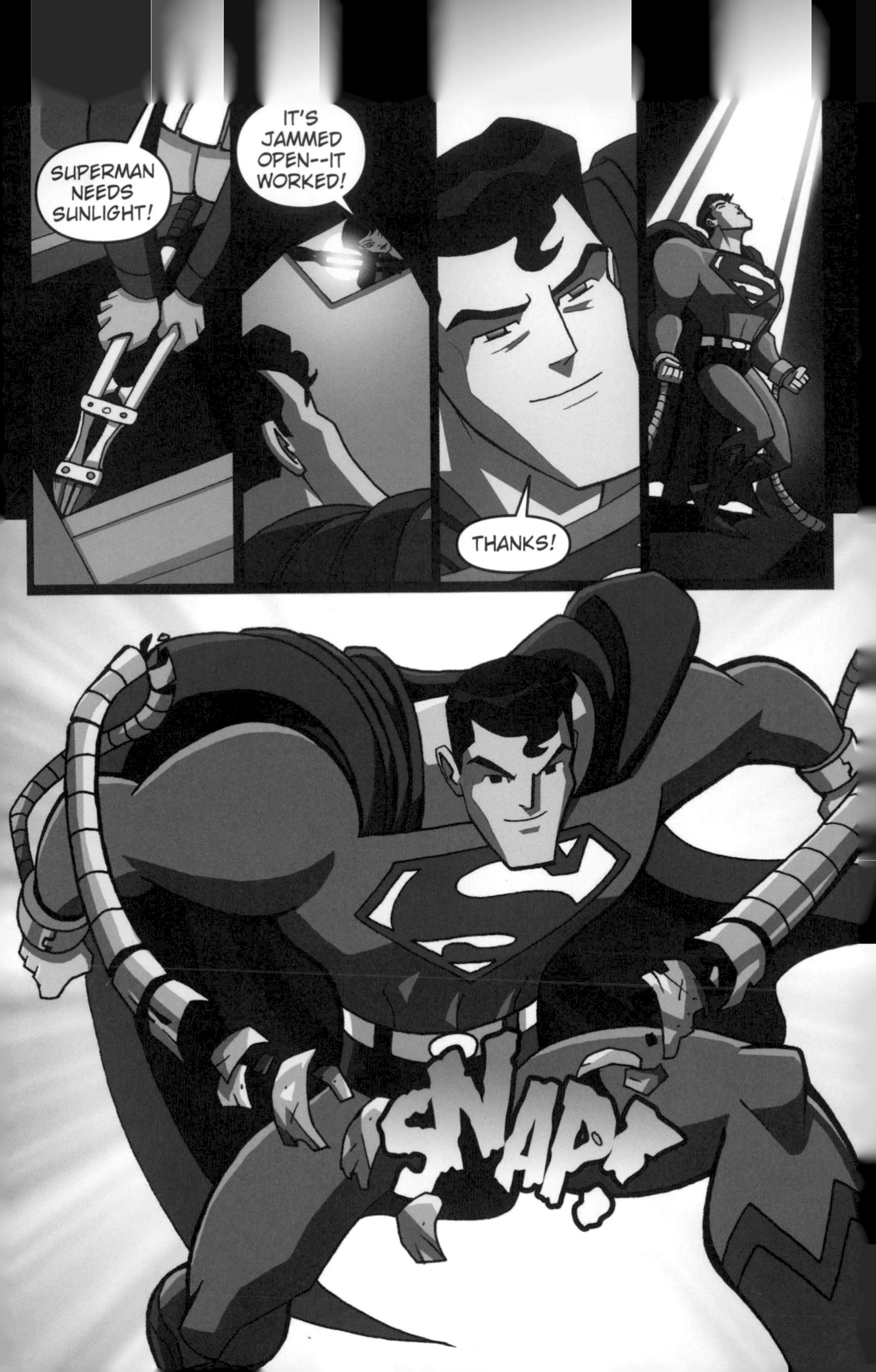
SUPERMAN NEEDS SUNLIGHT!
IT'S JAMMED OPEN--IT WORKED!
THANKS!
SNAP!

Superman was strong enough to break free. But he'd need to be much stronger to stop the Parasite. He remained motionless, drinking in the remaining sliver of sunlight.

Superman looked up through the skylight and met eyes with Lois. His eyes began to crackle with red energy. Lois nodded and grabbed Jimmy. "Come on!" she yelled.

THUMP THUMP THUMP THUMP THUMP THUMP

Superman followed the sound of Lois and Jimmy's footsteps as they dashed across the roof. He heard them leap onto the wind deflector, then slide down to the hood.

When Superman knew it was safe, he blasted upward with heat vision.

The roof of his prison melted into slag. Sunlight filled the container.

The Parasite, swollen and hideous, whirled. He held their nearly drained masked captor in his hands.

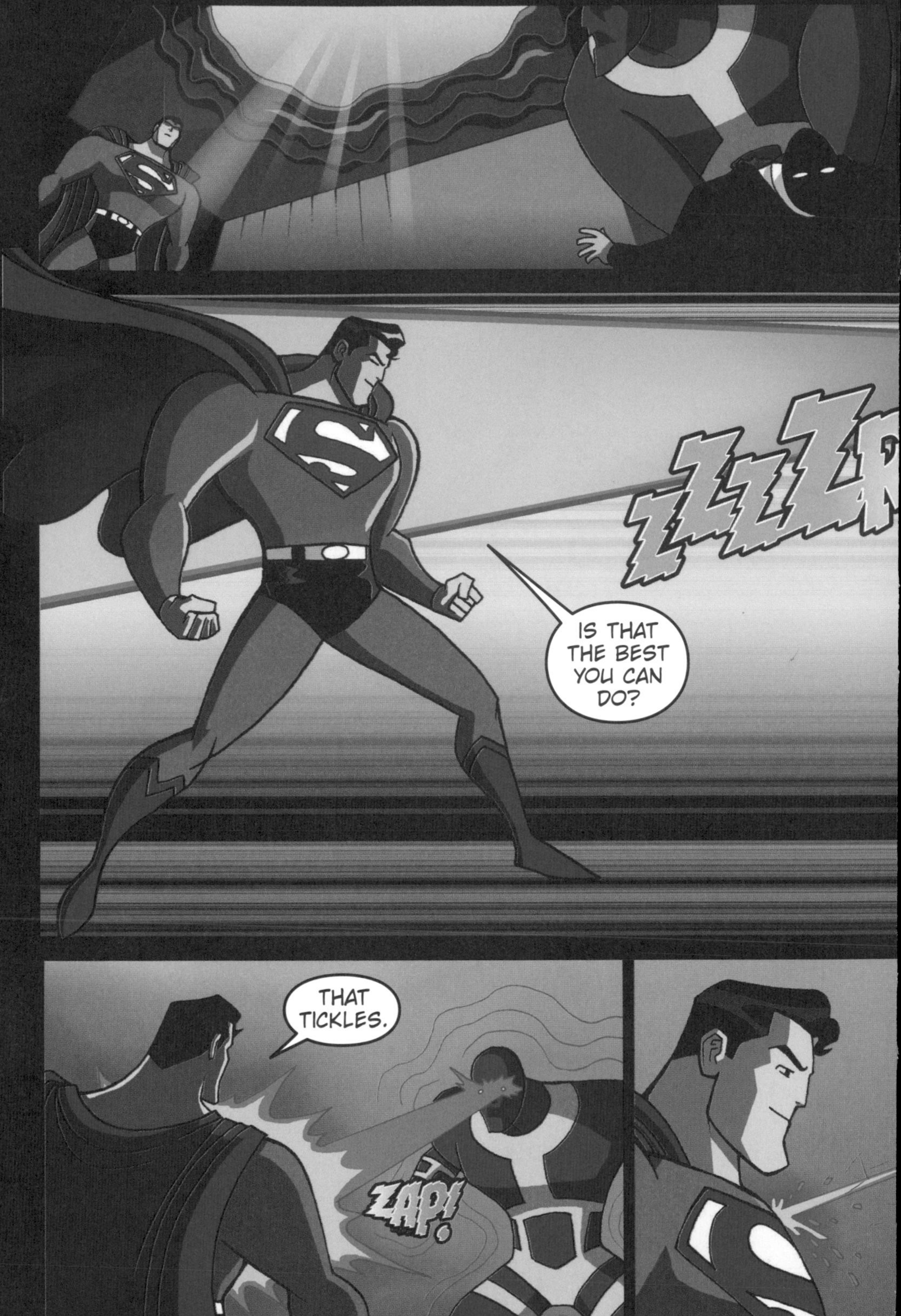
ZZZZR
IS THAT THE BEST YOU CAN DO?
THAT TICKLES.
ZAP!

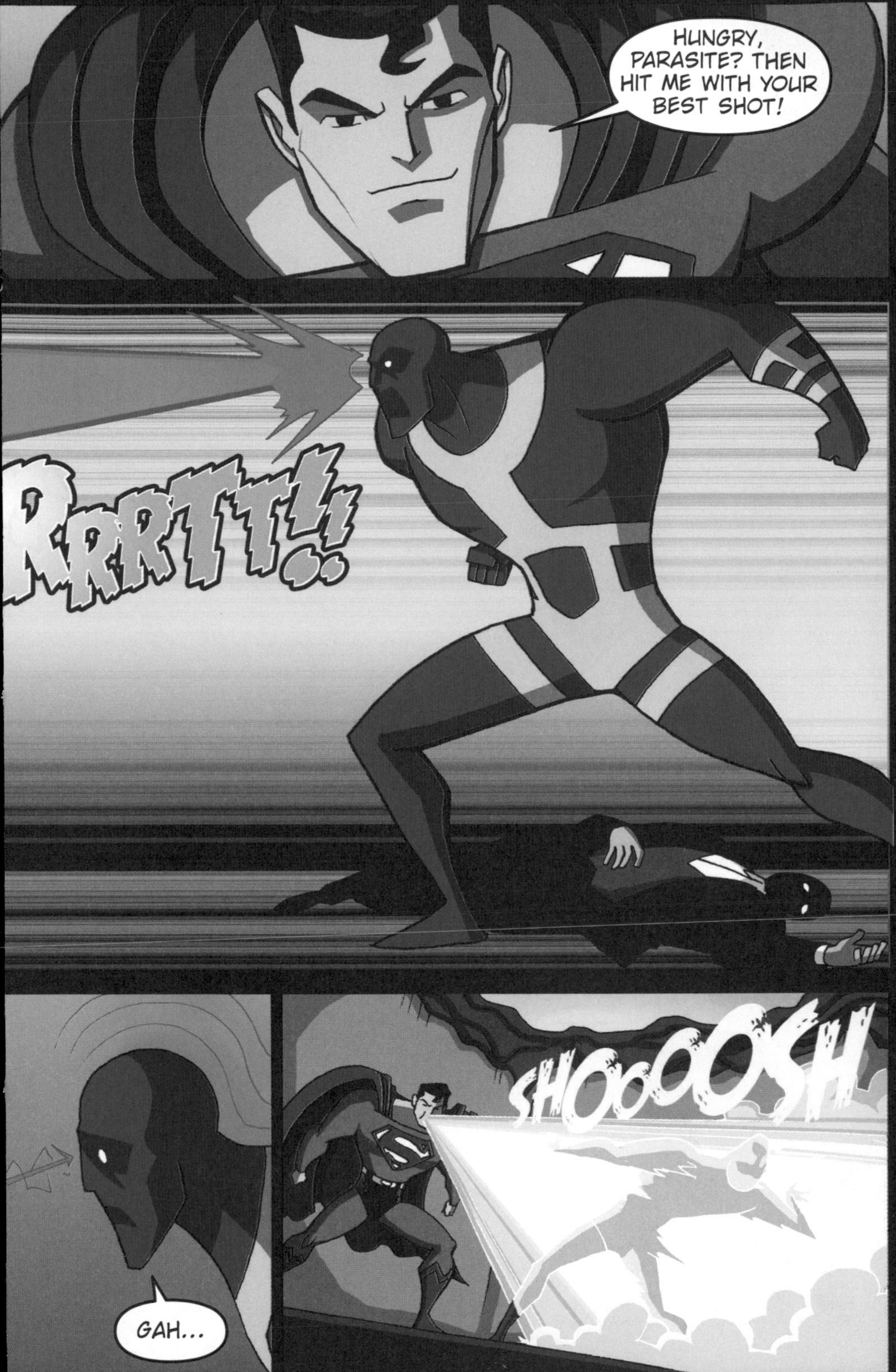
HUNGRY, PARASITE? THEN HIT ME WITH YOUR BEST SHOT!
RRRTT!!
GAH...
SHOOOOOSH

When Superman's freeze breath struck the Parasite, a sheet of frost formed around the monster. Soon the Parasite was imprisoned in a thick block of ice.

Finally, it was over.

Superman looked around. The rear door of the compartment was open. While he fought the Parasite, the masked leader and his guards had escaped.

LATER...

Superman stepped onto the loading dock as a fleet of police cars screeched into the parking lot. Lois and Jimmy rushed to him.

"The goons dragged their masked leader out," Lois said. "A van picked them up, but the masked man got away. I just know that man was Lex Luthor."

"It's odd," Superman said. "Like Lex, I have power — he has his money, I have my abilities. But I constantly feel the need to use my powers to keep the people of Metropolis safe while Lex takes advantage of them." Superman paused. "And when I was trapped without my powers, I realized nothing stood in Lex's way anymore . . ."

"That's not true," Lois said. "You had one power left . . ."

Superman tilted his head. "I did?"

"The power of friendship!" Lois said with a wink. "It goes both ways, you know. You've saved us tons of times. It was our turn to save you."

"So how did you stop the Parasite?" Jimmy asked.

"I put him on ice," Superman said. "And now I'm going to deliver him to Stryker's Island prison. As long as he's there, he won't be a drain on society."

Lois groaned at the Man of Steel's puns. Jimmy chuckled. Superman smiled and carried Parasite away.

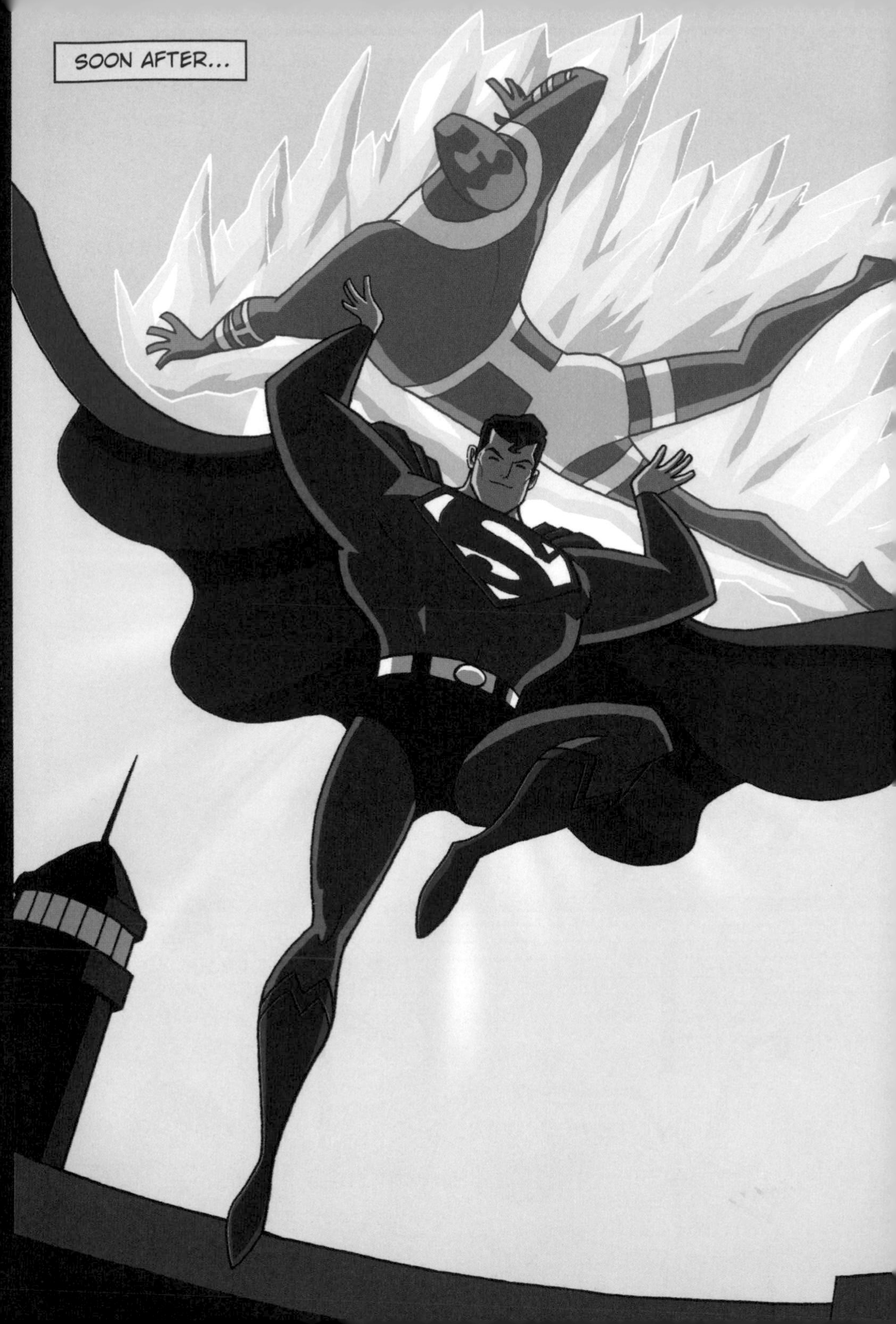
SOON AFTER...

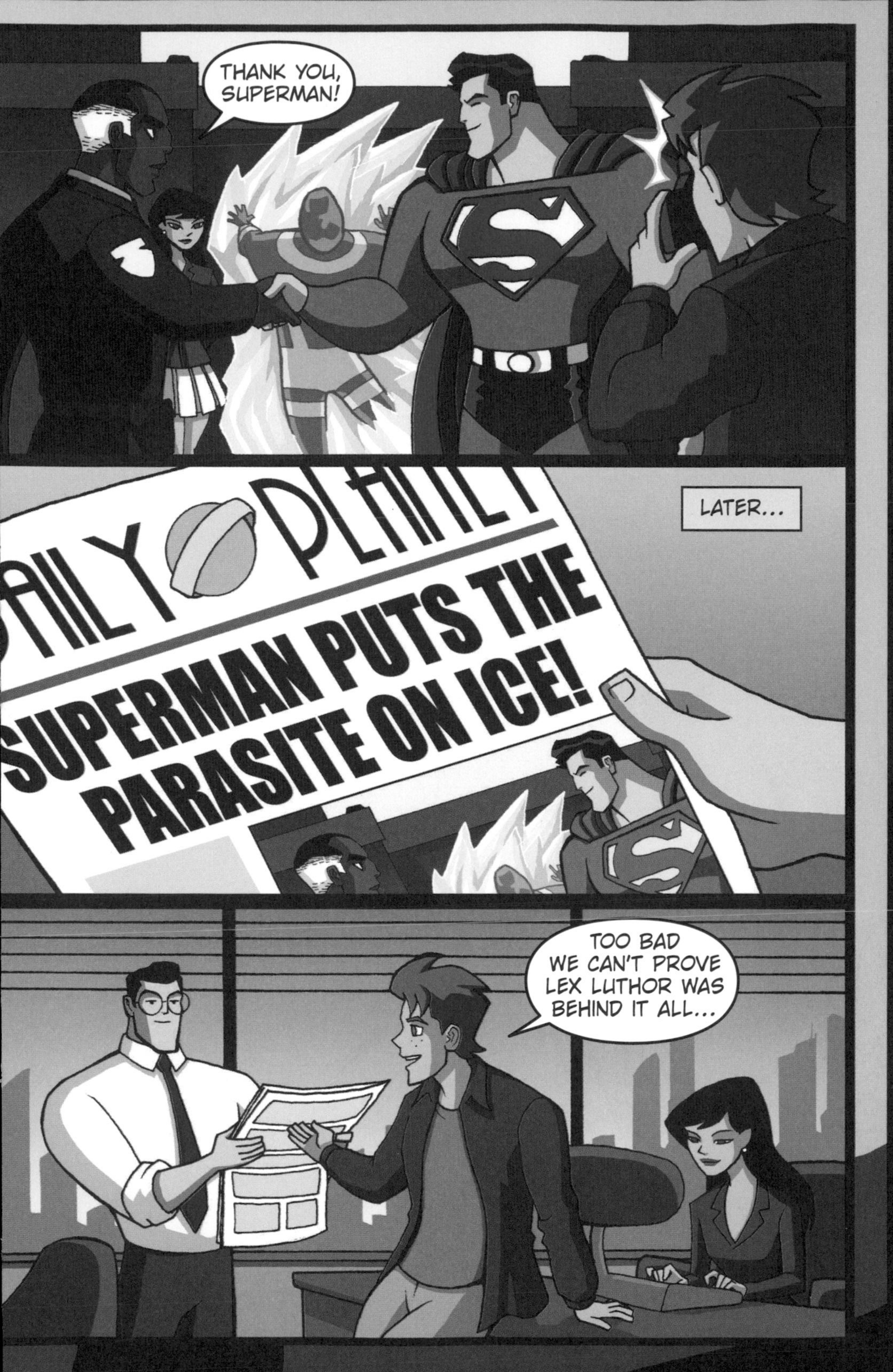
THANK YOU, SUPERMAN!
LATER...
SUPERMAN PUTS THE PARASITE ON ICE!
TOO BAD WE CAN'T PROVE LEX LUTHOR WAS BEHIND IT ALL...

"... but at least we found the rest of the Hammerz!" Jimmy finished.

"How did you manage to do that?" Clark asked.

"I told the police what I'd learned about the warehouse," Lois said. "They found crates of Hammerz hidden in the basement."

"To the surprise of no one," Jimmy added, "Luthor has managed to wiggle his way out of taking any blame for any of it."

Lois nodded and frowned. "He claimed he was sick and staying in a private hospital this whole time, so he didn't know what was happening. Had witnesses and everything," she said. "He looks so weak and pale that the cops believed him."

Clark nodded. "Being drained by the Parasite will do that to you," Clark murmured. "I mean, so I've been told," he added quickly.

"Luthor admitted he had designed the Hammerz, but meant for them to be non-lethal stun weapons used to incapacitate criminals," Lois continued. "He said he planned to offer them free of charge to police forces around the country. And, of course, he said he was horrified when he found out they'd fallen into the hands of criminals. But we all know that his cover story is a bunch of baloney."

"Yeah," Jimmy said glumly. "I think he wanted to supply the bad guys *and* the cops. That's a lot of Hammerz sold. And a lot of money that ultimately ends up in Luthor's pockets."

Clark patted his friends on their backs. "Cheer up, you two. After all, you both saved Superman's life!" Clark said. "And next time I know you'll catch Luthor in the act."

Jimmy smiled. "I sure hope so," he said.

Lois grinned and elbowed Clark in the ribs. "Maybe next time you'll lend a hand instead of sitting in the office twiddling your thumbs!" she added.

Clark grinned. "Maybe," he said.

BIOGRAPHIES

Louise Simonson writes about monsters, science fiction and fantasy characters, and super heroes. She wrote the award-winning Power Pack series, several best-selling X-Men titles, Web of Spider-man for Marvel Comics, and Superman: Man of Steel and Steel for DC Comics. She has also written many books for kids. She is married to comic artist and writer Walter Simonson and lives in the suburbs of New York City.

Luciano Vecchio was born in 1982 and currently lives in Buenos Aires, Argentina. With experience in illustration, animation, and comics, his works have been published in the US, Spain, the UK, France, and Argentina. His credits include Ben 10 (DC Comics), Cruel Thing (Norma), Unseen Tribe (Zuda Comics), and Sentinels (Drumfish Productions).

SKETCHES

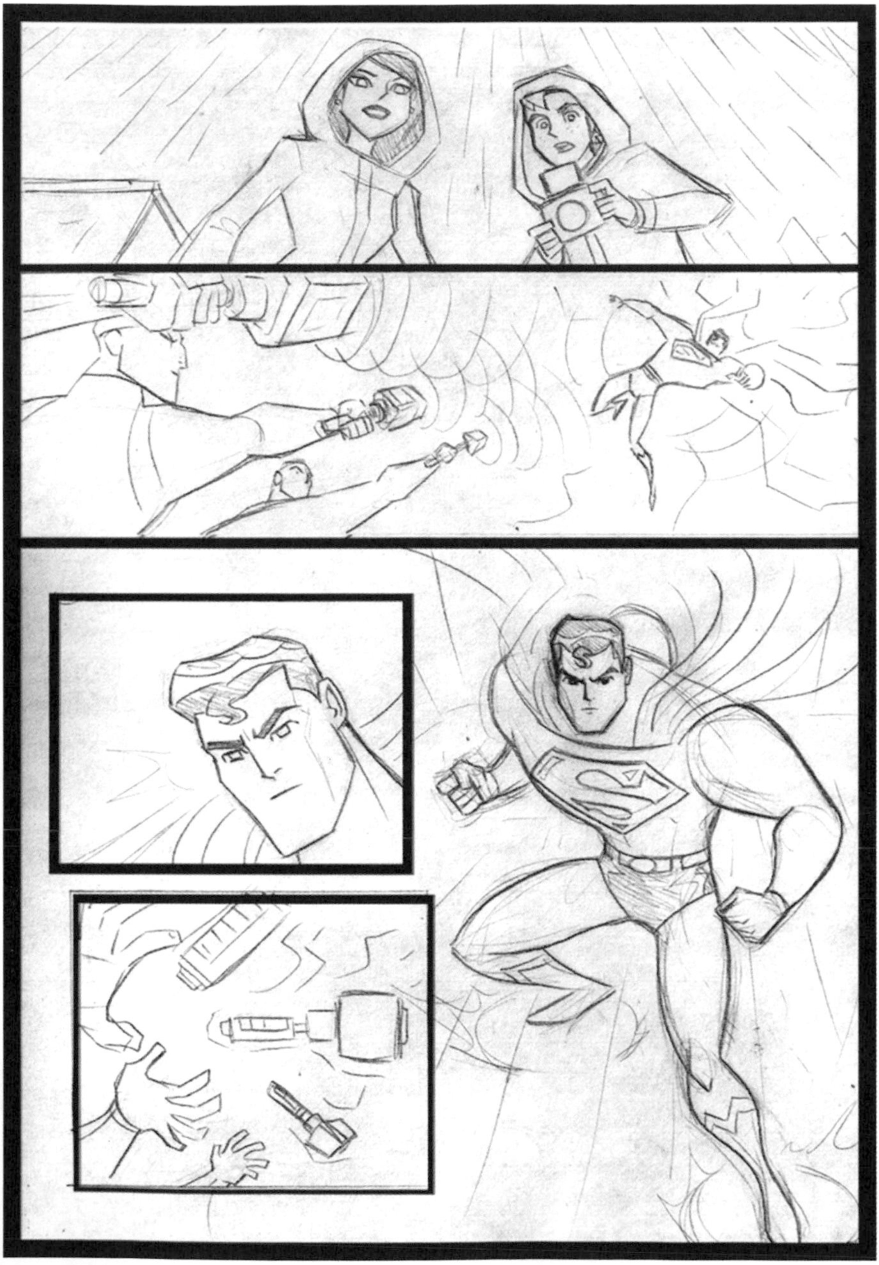

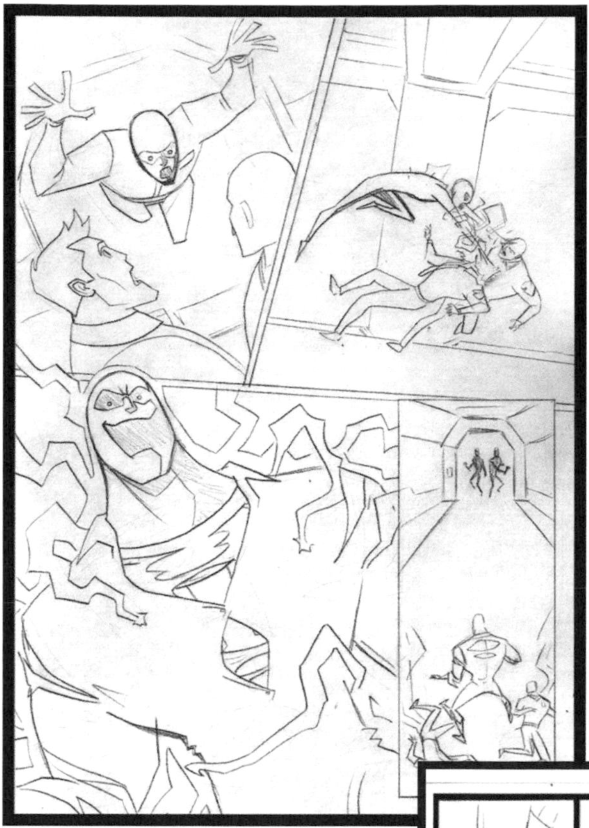

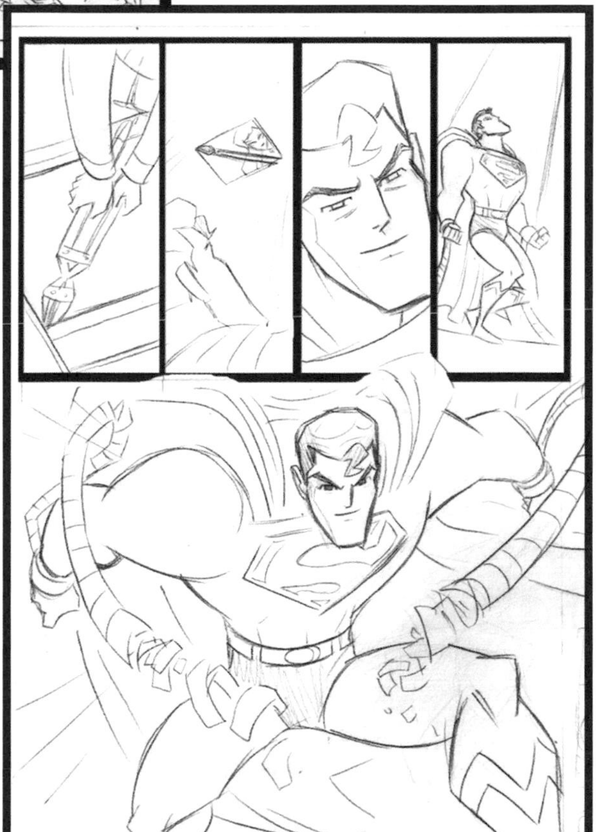

FINAL ART

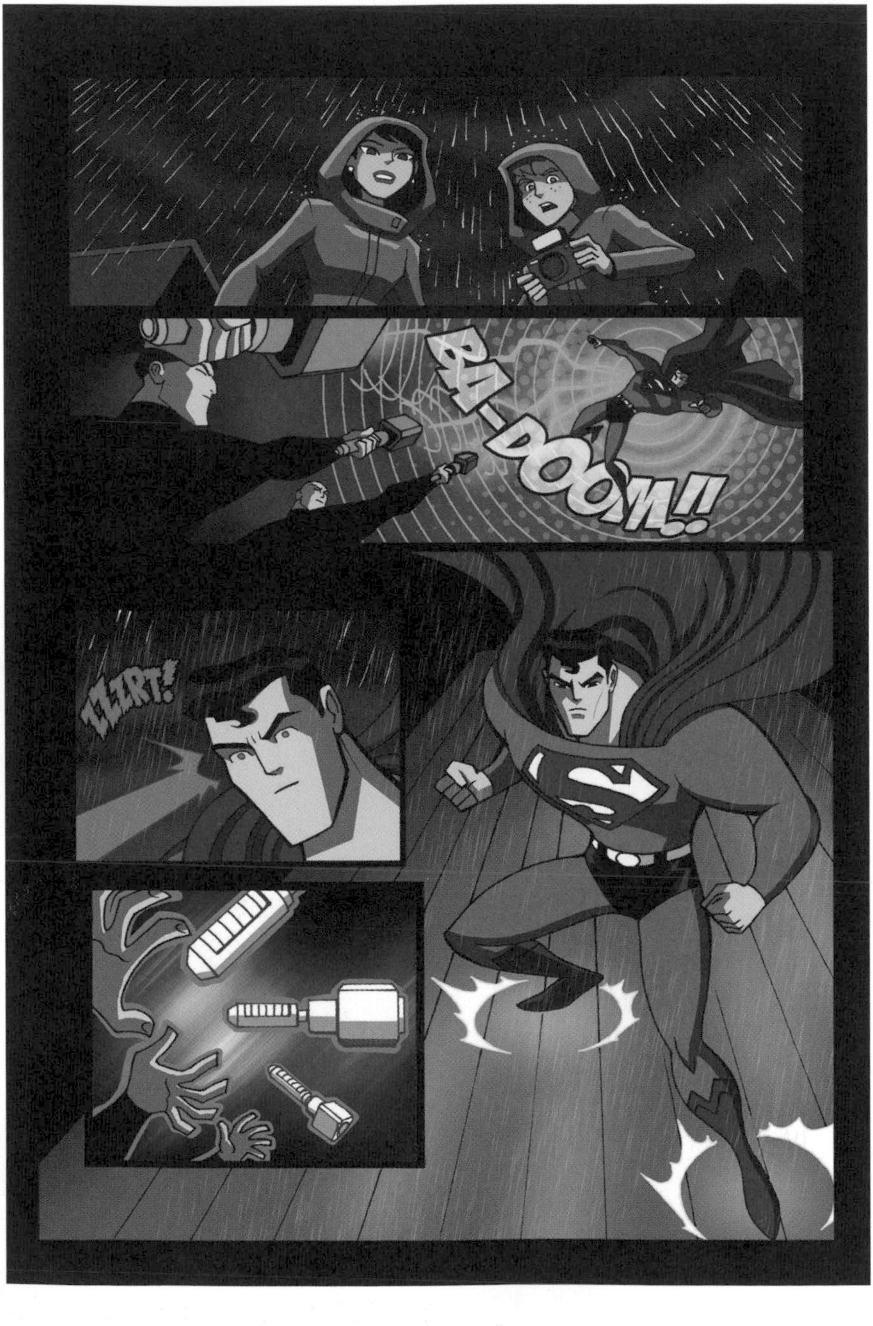
BA-DOOM!!
ZZZRT!

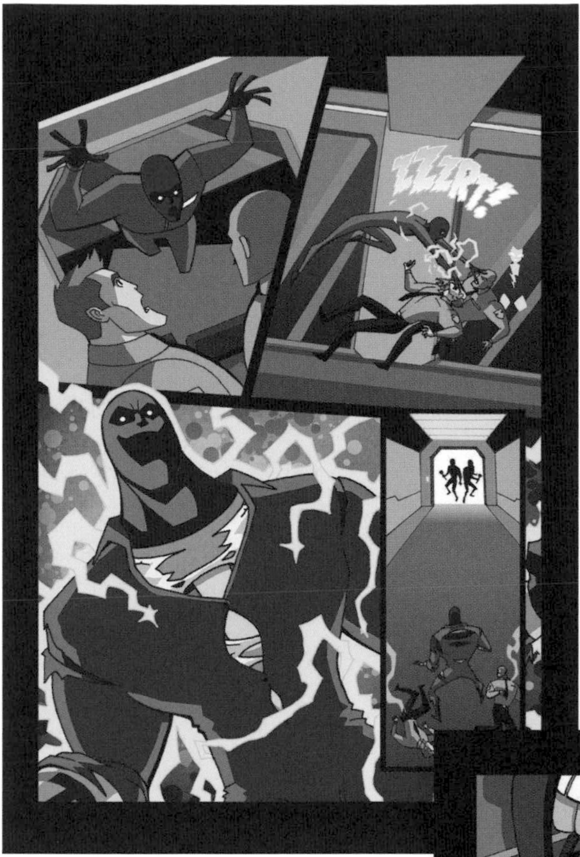
ZZZRT!

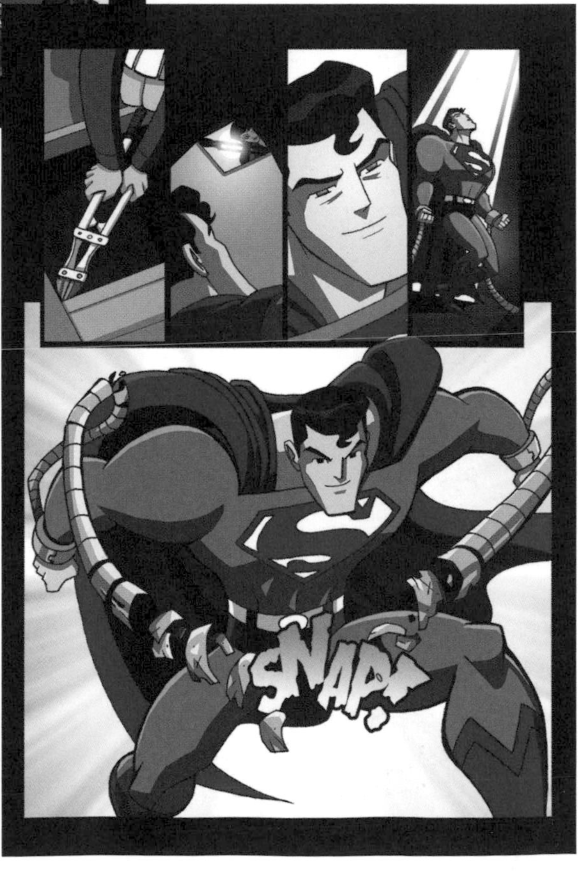
SNAP!

COMICS TERMS

caption (KAP-shuhn)—words that appear in a box. Captions are often used to set the scene.

gutter (GUHT-er)—the space between panels or pages

motion lines (MOH-shuhn LINES)—illustrator-created marks that help show motion in art

panel (PAN-uhl)—a single drawing that has borders around it. Each panel is a separate scene on a spread.

SFX (ESS-EFF-EKS)—short for sound effects. Sound effects are words used to show sounds that occur in the art of a comic.

splash (SPLASH)—a large illustration that often covers a full page (or more)

spread (SPRED)—two side-by-side pages in a comic book

word balloon (WURD BUH-loon)—a speech indicator that includes a character's dialogue or thoughts. A word balloon's tail leads to the speaking character's mouth.

GLOSSARY

buffeted (BUHF-i-tid)—hit something with great force many times

disperse (di-SPERSS)—to go in different directions or spread apart

evading (i-VAY-ding)—escaping through trickery or cleverness

freak (FREEK)—something unusual or unexpected

invulnerable (in-VUHL-nuhr-uh-buhl)—impossible to harm, damage, or defeat

meddling (MED-ling)—becoming involved in the activities and concerns of other people when your involvement is not wanted

pier (PEER)—a structure that goes out from the shore into the water

proposal (pruh-POH-zuhl)—a plan or suggestion presented to someone

smuggling (SMUHGL-ing)—moving something from one place to another illegally

withered (WITH-urd)—thin and wrinkled because of old age or weakness

VISUAL QUESTIONS

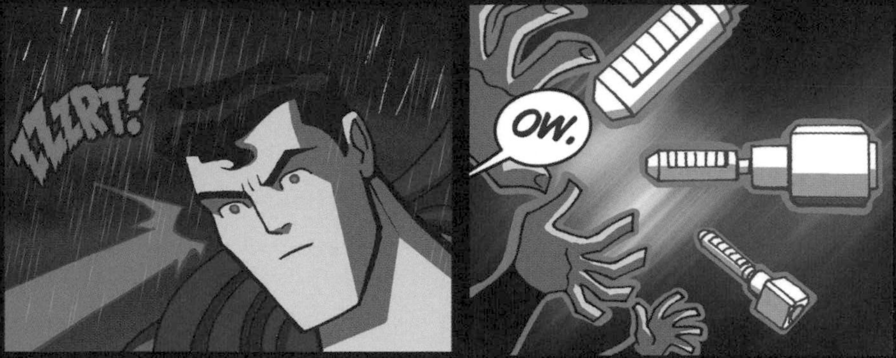

ZZZRT!
OW.

1. In your own words explain what happens in these two panels. Read the rest of page 14 for clues.

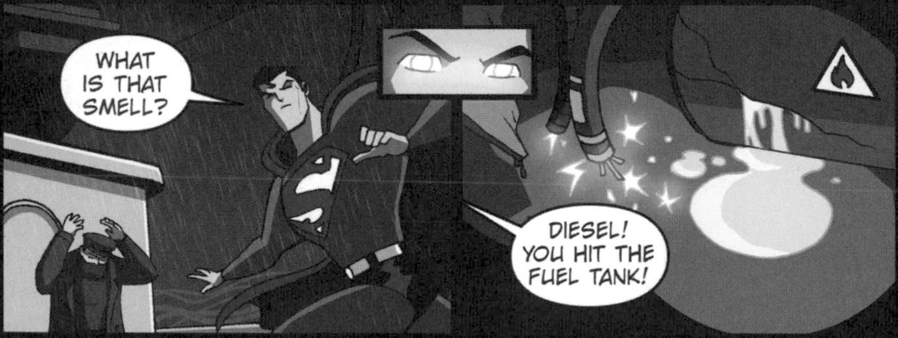

WHAT IS THAT SMELL?
DIESEL! YOU HIT THE FUEL TANK!

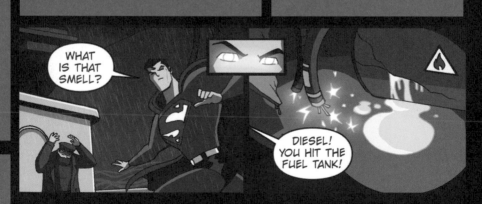

2. What is happening in this sequence of panels? What did Superman learn? How did he learn it?

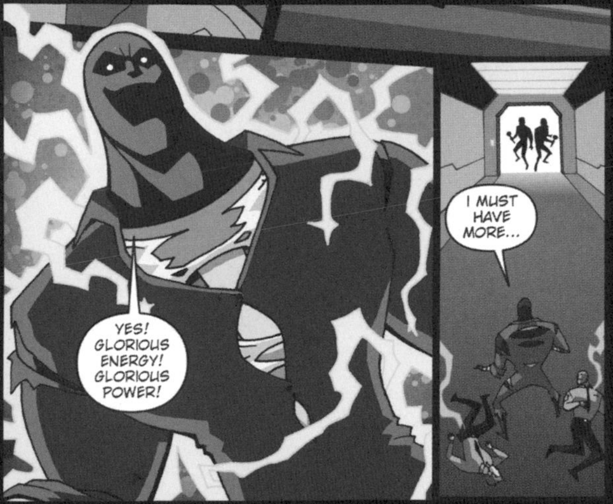
YES! GLORIOUS ENERGY! GLORIOUS POWER!
I MUST HAVE MORE...

3. What is happening to Parasite here? What details in the art explain what is happening?

4. What was Lois's plan to free Superman? How did she know it would work?

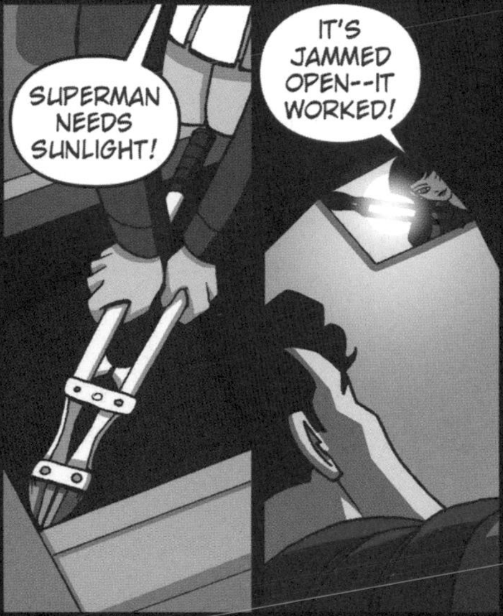
SUPERMAN NEEDS SUNLIGHT!
IT'S JAMMED OPEN--IT WORKED!

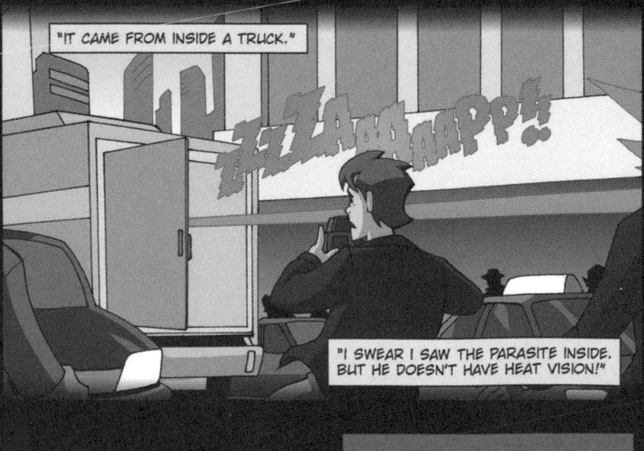
"IT CAME FROM INSIDE A TRUCK."
ZZZZAAAAAPP!!
"I SWEAR I SAW THE PARASITE INSIDE. BUT HE DOESN'T HAVE HEAT VISION!"

5. Why are the two panels colored differently than the rest? Why does Jimmy's speech appear in captions instead of dialogue balloons?

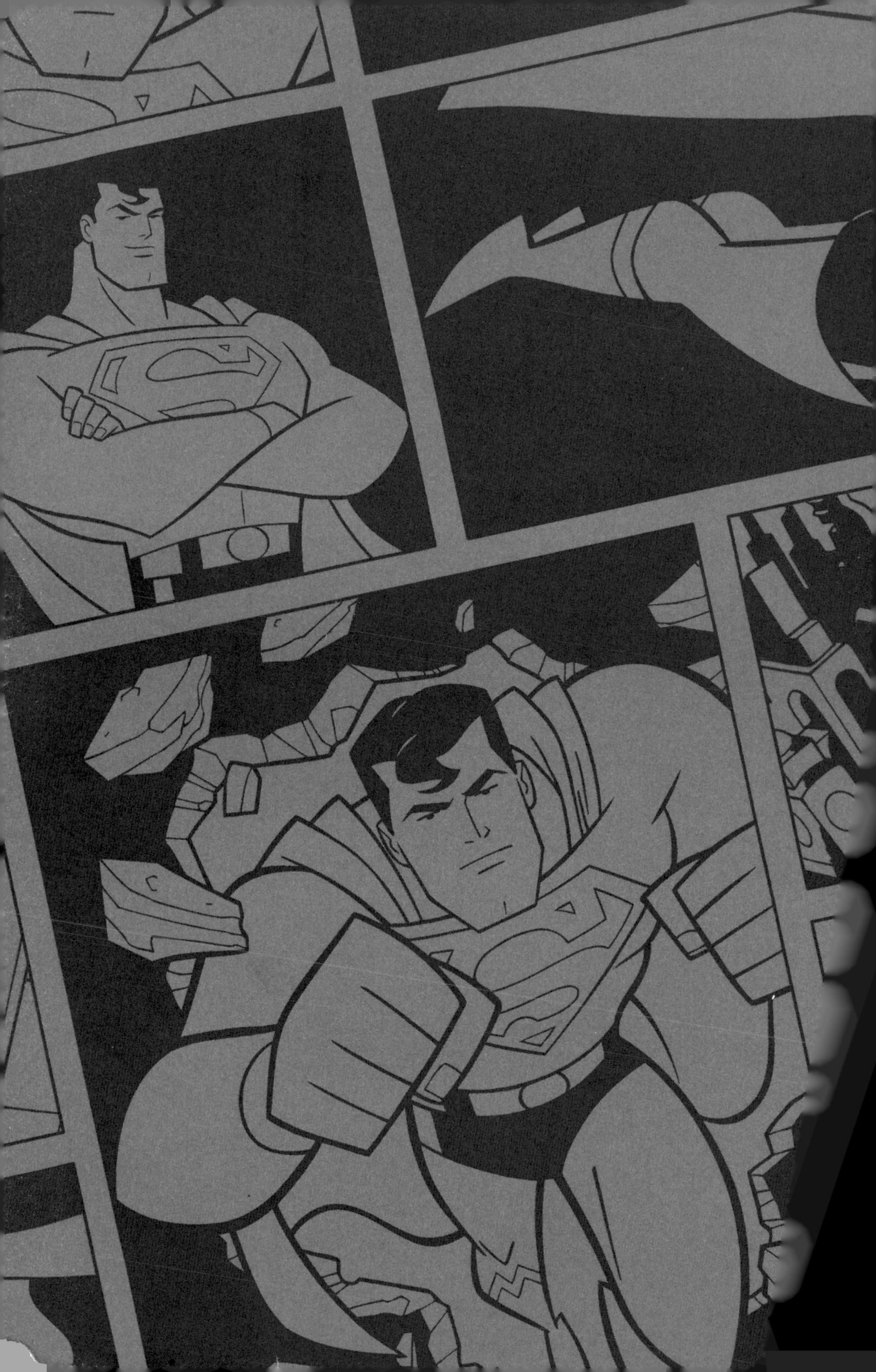

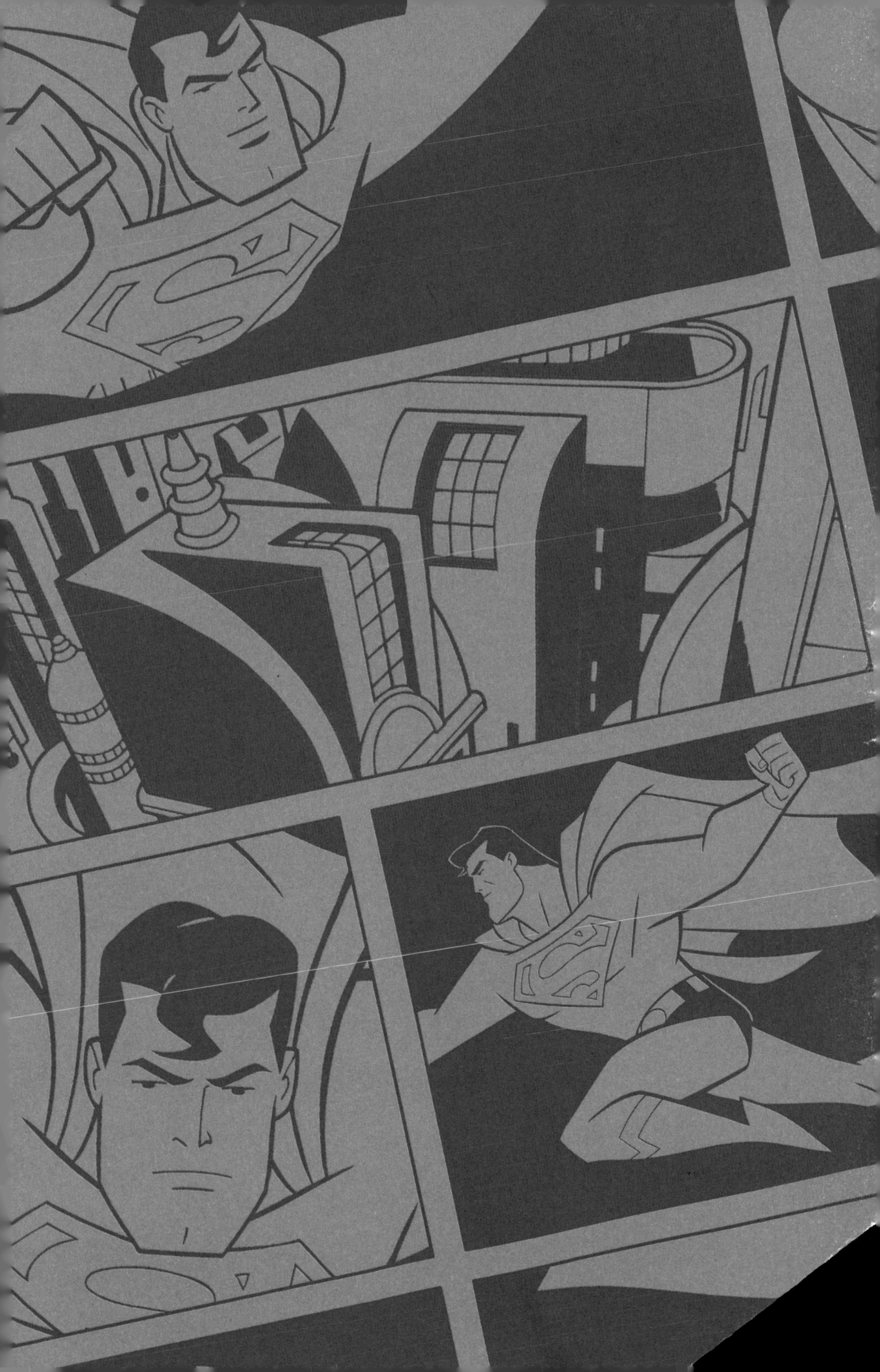